TALES TO RAISE ADULT HUMANS BY

TS Kummelman

The characters and events portrayed in this book are fictitious. Seriously. Any similarity to real persons, entities, space tentacles, immortal evil corporate bastards, or yoga instructors, living or dead, is coincidental and not intended by the author.

ISBN-13: 978-1-7352447-3-0

Cover design by: Bruce Rolff
Library of Congress Control Number: 2020911692
Printed in the United States of America (but please don't judge the rest of the country based on the crappy writing in this book)

"Broken Books" originally published in HAUNTED BY THE PAST, Tacitus Publishing, 2016

"Space Cookies" originally published in SHATTERED SPACE, Tacitus Publishing, 2017

For Brandon and Hayley
While I tried to raise you both with a sense of wonder and imagination, please, don't let this book interfere with your dreams. Seriously. You can do better than this crap!

CONTENTS

Title Page	1
Copyright	2
Dedication	3
BROKEN BOOKS	7
MARY, VERIFIED	31
THE EVIL END	53
THE GREAT OFFICE MELEE OF 1973	63
ANDREA'S PROBABILITY	87
BULLETS AND TIME	107
Interlude: Bob the Dog	118
BLOOD WORK FOR MORTON	121
BIWITCHED	132
THE FINE ART OF DYING	160
SPACE COOKIES	186
BALANCING AFTER	218
A WORKOUT FOR THE AGES	235
epilogue	271

Acknowledgments 274
About The Author 279

BROKEN BOOKS

"A book?" Jacob Harker said into the telephone, incredulous at the idea.

"And why not?" exclaimed Ward on the other end.

His voice came across as scratchy and distant, difficult to catch everything said. Harker was not comfortable with this new technology. He still felt the need for human interaction over some ethereal device. Speaking to his friend and occasional employer, Phineas Ward, about a haunted book did nothing at all to calm him while trying to deal with a disembodied voice in his ear.

"If dolls, houses, and people can be abused by the afterlife, why not a book? Makes perfect sense, if you ask me. Which you did not . . . which is why I'm still talking. Harker, are you there?"

"Yes, yes," he answered, "still here. It's just . . ."

There was a click on the line, and there

was another voice. "Oh, ah . . . hello? Is someone on the line?"

"Yes, ma'am," Ward said. "So please get off."

"Well, I need to use the tellyphone. How long have you been on it?"

Harker sighed, knowing what was coming next.

"It does not matter in the least how long we've been on it," Ward stated. "You are interrupting a private conversation. Whoever you are, please hang up on your end and try again in ten minutes." The irritation in his voice was unmistakable. The man had little love for anyone he considered to be below his mental stature, which was, insofar as Ward was concerned, everyone else on the planet.

"I'll not hang up," the lady said.

"It's rude to interrupt a private conversation, madam. Is that not your thought, too, Jacob?"

"'Tis a bit rude," Harker agreed.

"Thank you. Now, madam, please hang up."

"I'm a *sir*."

"What?"

"That's three times now you've called me *madam*; I am a *sir*."

"Well, you sound like a madam. Jacob, does he not sound like a woman?"

"Interrupts like one, too," Harker

agreed.

"Jacob, please just meet me at the location I mentioned. I'll not say it again, for fear of a mystery *person* further interrupting our conversation."

"Man," said the oddly feminine voice. "I am a man."

Harker smiled. "I'll see you there in an hour." As he was hanging up the receiver, he could distinctly hear Ward saying, "And a good day to you, too . . . madam."

* * *

The Belmont Library was located just north of South Kensington. Harker marveled at the town's growth as he stepped off the train. Where once had been open fields and farms, buildings now rose out of the ground in large swaths, roads crisscrossed, and noise filled the scene.

He'd spent a summer here in the '50s with his parents at the estate of a family friend. The English countryside had fascinated him as a boy, and he'd been looking forward to returning with his own family one day. Fate had seen otherwise; his first wife had died during childbirth, and the second had . . . well, the rumor in London was that she'd run off with a ship's captain to America, but that was never confirmed.

But now, in this, the early years of the 1900's, he saw not the carefully tended estates or farms of his childhood, but development. He was happy for what the various businesses and industries did to better all of England, but after being in The City for four decades straight, he'd been looking forward to a break from the hustle and sounds of city living. Even if he was here on what was essentially a ghost hunt.

Sighing, Harker picked up the satchel at his feet and headed through the crowded station. Even the station itself looked new, from the polished wood floors to the tiled walls. He imagined as he passed families stepping off the train that they were just beginning their vacations, and the others waiting to board ending their own. He was marveling at the tile work of the entryway when a familiar voice called to him from the street. Harker spied Ward bounding up the steps, his own briefcase in his hand, his long coat billowing out behind him.

Phineas Ward was a tall, lanky fellow, much unlike Harker's short, stocky build. To him, Ward was a true sign of The City's elite. Thin and well kept. His clothes were neatly pressed and his hair immaculate and neat. The only thing which set him apart from the aforementioned crowd was the color of his skin; Ward was a black man. And while he acted like everyone else, spoke with an educated air, and dressed with the utmost sense of fashion, it was this but this one singular difference which, on occasion, made his life more difficult than it should have been. But Harker knew that under the dark, tough skin and the carefully nurtured air of bourgeois was a firm grip, a quick wit, and one of the keenest brains in London.

"Jacob!" Ward nearly bowled his friend over, clasping him and nearly crushing off his oxygen supply with a hug. "So good to see you, my friend."

Smiling, Harker took a step back to compose himself. "It has been too long, Mr. Ward. We should see each other more often; leastways, my suit may fare better upon reunions."

Ward laughed, then guided him to an awaiting carriage. "It is but a brief ride to the library, so we've not much time to catch up. Perhaps tonight we can reacquaint ourselves over some lamb and brandy, but for now—" he pulled open the door and bowed, sweeping his arm inward, ". . . thy chariot awaits."

Ward gave him the details during the short, bumpy jaunt. What he knew was clearly short on particulars.

"Within the library is one specific book

which, when removed from the shelf, repeatedly opens to the same page."

Harker looked back at him, mouth agape.

"That is what you called me all the way out here for?"

Ward's grin wavered.

"Do not mistake me, I enjoy a holiday as much as any working man, but a book that opens to the same page? Sincerely? It has to be the binding, friend, nothing more."

His companion waved away his answer and scoffed. "Do you not think that was the first explanation to occur to me? However, the librarian assured me that the binding is weathered the same throughout. It is not a very old edition, and, while it may be prone to some discoloration cosmetically, and some folded pages and torn binding physically, there is little scientific evidence that explains the pages turning by themselves."

Harker thought on it for a moment—just long enough for the hansom to pull up to the stone steps of the library. As they exited and Ward flipped the driver a florin, Harker noted the stonework of the building itself. It was an old building, but one he did not recall from his youth. Surely it had been here during his previous trip. The structure was the only one on the street not made of wood. It was three stories in height, with stained glass adorning the windows along the top floor, gargoyles situated along the corners of the tiled roof, and the words "Belmont Library" etched into the stones above the door in a distinct and very unusual script.

"Lovely building, is it not?"

Harker looked at Ward, judging his tone and facial set as lacking any sarcasm. It was, indeed, a fine-looking library.

"Shall we?"

* * *

The librarian was small and portly and looked more like a prissy banker than he did a caretaker of books. Yet, Harker discovered that the man's love for the tomes was self-evident in the way he looked upon and spoke of them. Even when it came to the edition in question, which the man stoutly refused to touch, one could see he also cared for that which he feared.

Having walked them up to the second floor, the small man explained, "I'd keep it on the third, but it is a popular edition, and I've enough to do without having to climb three flights every other day." The librarian brought them directly to the shelf and nodded to the books aligned there. Harker had been trying to pay attention to the layout of the aisles, but the sheer number of books, and the height of the shelves themselves, had him flabbergasted. He could think of no other place he would rather spend his holiday than walking each and every aisle, every one seemingly equipped with a stepping stool to reach the highest shelves, of this wondrous building.

"There it is," the librarian said, pointing at a row of carefully placed books. Even with every space filled, this book stood out from the others, in that there was an inch gap to either side.

"Why are no other books with it?" Ward inquired. There were other novels by the same author on either side, and from Harker's knowledge of the writer, he saw that no editions were missing.

"Because the book will not allow others to touch it."

The companions each raised an inquisitive eyebrow to the librarian, who merely shrugged. "Experiment all you like, gentlemen, but if you damage this or any other book in any way . . ." When he said this, Harker noted the sidelong glance the man made at Ward, as though the black man could not be trusted amongst such precious items.

Ward shook his head but made no indication that he had been offended by the librarian's unease. "No worries, good sir. I assure you that myself and Mr. Harker have the utmost respect for the written word, and would never see any harm come to them."

The short man eyed them both, shrugged, then motioned to the end of the aisle. "There are tables and chairs in the sitting area. The library closes at seven, so you have several hours to make of your investigation." With that, he left them both to stare at the book which sat alone in a crowded room of thousands.

After a few moments had passed, Ward reached up and pushed the books on either side up against the volume in question. They watched intently, waiting to see the leather spines pushed apart by an invisible force. Yet nothing happened.

They looked at each other and smiled. *"The book will not allow others to touch it,"* Ward mimicked. Yet when they both looked back, the volume again sat alone, the other volumes having been moved aside.

Harker swallowed, and in the silence of the second floor of the Belmont Library, the sound seemed to echo.

After a few moments of simply staring at it, Ward inquired, "Surely the title of the book is inconsequential . . ?"

"I suppose we shall soon find that out," Harker replied, and pulled Fyodor Dostoevsky's *Bésy* from the shelf.

* * *

"Do it again."

They stood, staring down at the book, which was opened to page four hundred and twenty-two. The Russian words stared back up at them, almost accusatory. They had tried, unsuccessfully, to get the book to stay open to both prior and later pages, all to no avail. Unlike the moving of the other books, there were no hidden machinations or unwitnessed phenomena when it came to the tome *adjusting itself*, as Ward had coined the phrase ten minutes ago.

Harker sighed, reached out, and shut the book. Then he re-opened it to a page somewhere in the six-hundreds. As soon as his fingers left the proximity of the volume, the pages flipped past in a blur—and stopped at page four hundred and twenty-two.

Other experiments had ended in the same way. Shut the book completely, and it flipped open, exactly to that page. Close it and stand it up on the table, it would fall over, then open itself. Right at page four hundred and twenty-two. They had tried turning it upside down, walking away and ignoring it for twenty minutes—nothing different ever occurred.

"I'm not sure it is the book itself which is possessed," Ward murmured.

"How so? Does it not open itself to the same page every time?" As far as Harker was concerned, this was an item touched by an otherworldly spirit. "It would seem to me that the book is quite impressed with its own page four hundred and twenty-two."

"Firstly, the other books. I would think an outside presence would be necessary to physically move the other books away from it. Otherwise, the book itself would have to physically push the others aside, and we know that is not happening." Half an hour ago, they had placed a scrap of paper atop the book while it was on the shelf and then pushed other volumes up against it. When they turned back around, the paper scrap had not moved; the other books had.

"Secondly, as far as physics are concerned, can you see a book pushing itself over? It has no musculature, no sense of gravity unless it is pushed or thrown . . ."

"What of the doll in Lancashire fifteen years ago, then? Are you implying there was a hidden circulatory system within the stuffing?"

Ward smirked, still staring down at the book. "Of course not. You know yourself that was possessed by a demon, as we were able to trap it in a bottle."

Harker recalled that experience all too well. He still refused to drink from a bottle because of it.

"How is a book written in Russian any different than a child's toy stuffed with cotton?"

"Because a doll, no matter how inhuman it looks, is still fashioned after a human. A book is not."

"Although a book is usually about humans—at least this one is."

Ward looked away from the book for the first time in the last hour, and did so in a sheepish manner. He muttered something about the title being the Russian word for demon, which left Harker exasperated.

"You've never read this book, have you?" Harker asked. A timid shake of the head was all the answer he needed. "Dear Lord, man! And here I thought you were an expert on everything!"

Ward looked back and said, with no little amount of defensiveness, "It is a Russian writing about demons—what would a Russian know about demons that we do not already know from *The Bible*?!"

Harker shook his head. "It is not a book about demons, friend. It is a book about men who become something akin to demons, how their actions and disassociation with morality turn them into horrible, horrible people. It is not about demons in the biblical sense, rather in the metaphorical and psychological sense."

Ward glanced down at the book, then back up to his friend's eyes. "Well, I do not read Russian now, do I?"

Harker, for once glad to have the advantage on his brilliant companion, straightened his collar, sat down in front of the book, and cleared his throat. It had been a decade since he'd last read the controversial novel.

After reading a few lines in Russian aloud, the book suddenly snapped shut.

Harker, for all of his pride and poise, let out a squeak and, frightened, pushed away from the table. As he stared at the book, it suddenly re-opened itself. To page four hundred and twenty-two, of course.

"What in the name of . . ."

"Here, try that again," Ward said.

Harker shook his head. "The damnable thing nearly took off my nose! If you think . . ."

His friend held up a hand, smiling gently. "This time, translate it. Read it in English."

Confusion knitted Harker's brow until he understood. He drew the chair back up to the table, cleared his throat once again, and began to re-read what he had earlier spoken in Russian, this time translating it to English.

* * *

After a few hours, Harker could go no further. The light outside was beginning to fail, and his throat was tiring from the continuous reading.

Rubbing his eyes, he pushed back from the table, stretched, and was barely able to stifle a yawn. "I think that is enough for tonight," as he closed the book.

The book then promptly re-opened itself, but not to page four hundred and twenty-two. He had read all the way to five hundred and fifty-three, and it was that page to which the book was now opened.

He shook his head and looked about the room. "More tomorrow, I promise," he said, talking to the shadowed stacks.

With the book in hand, he returned it to the shelf, not bothering to push the other volumes up against it.

The librarian greeted them downstairs and inquired of their results. Ward gave him a brief, if not unsatisfactory explanation, not wanting to cloud the man's judgment or contaminate the process.

"Could you please do me two favors this evening?" Ward asked him. "We shall need the name of the person who last had this book out the longest, and, if you would be so kind, open the book later and write down which page it falls to."

The librarian, who appeared to be an expert shoulder shrugger, shrugged again, and said that he would comply. And again, Ward appeared to not notice the lingering glance from the librarian, at least not from what Harker could tell.

* * *

Over dinner, Ward and Harker talked about anything *except* the book. As promised earlier, they spent their time catching each other up on their lives, and reminiscing over prior escapades with both the paranormal and their various romantic rendezvous. Harker had considered asking his friend if the treatment from the librarian didn't bother him; his mind kept going back to the man's body language, and it nagged at him. He hated to see his friend treated in such a manner, but without outright cause, he knew there was little he could do to defend him. Although Ward never let on that he needed to be defended; he was a proud man, the son of sharecroppers whom had met their fates in Mississippi. He had told him before of his childhood, of being smuggled aboard a ship bound for Great Britain, and his subsequent adoption into a rich household in London.

But the undercurrent to his upbringing had always, ceaselessly, involved the bigotry of others. It was never so bad as the stories one heard of the slavery in America, yet the condescension and vulgarities, no matter how well they were wrapped in niceties, still bit to the core. Harker had seen it throughout his life, witnessed others being oppressed by bigotries and ignorance. And while he had never felt that hatred towards another human no matter their differences, be it class or race or religion, he still felt a pang of guilt whenever he witnessed anyone, most notably his dear friend, having to suffer at the verbal abuse of others.

Ultimately, he decided to not bring up the librarian's treatment. Ward was typically predisposed to speaking his mind, and would probably deal with the man's prejudice how he saw fit. It did not mean that Harker would not hurt for him in the meantime.

It was when they settled before the picturesque hearth in the spacious inn, brandy and cigars in hand, that they spoke of the current case. Ward was now insistent that the book itself was haunted.

"I was wrong, earlier. I think the book itself wants to be read aloud. Like its characters, I think that particular volume is so egotistical that it will only be sated when you read the last line on the final page."

Harker smiled and shook his head. "It is but a ghost, and I am willing to bet you dinner tomorrow night that I am correct and you are in the wrong."

"Bah," Ward responded. "That book is far too proud of itself, that's the problem."

Harker wondered if the evening liquors were clouding his friend's perception. "You yourself said that its lack of any muscles would preclude it from being able to open itself up."

"And if I recall, it was you who insisted the book seemed rather pleased with its own page four hundred and twenty-two," countered Ward.

Harker laughed. "Touché, my friend. We will just have to see tomorrow, won't we?"

"Just be glad of one thing, Jacob. At least the book wasn't a Tolstoy!"

* * *

The following morning, Harker and Ward arrived early in hopes of finishing by the evening.

"I have that information for you," the librarian said to Ward as they were passing the front desk, indicating a wooden platter at the end of the counter. The tray held a pitcher of water, two glasses, and two pieces of paper. On the first piece of paper was the number *553*.

"How did you get it to change to a different page?" the librarian inquired as Ward scanned the note. Harker noticed that the previous look of disdain was nowhere evident on his face today; clearly, he had a different impression of the black man, now that there had been progress.

"My good man, as I am sure you can hear, my friend here has been working his way through the novel. I am positive that by the time he finishes the book, you will no longer have any issues. Apparently, it wants to be heard."

Before the librarian could ask any further questions, Ward picked up the tray and headed to the wrought iron stairs which wound up to the second floor—effectively dismissing the man, and firmly establishing an unspoken hierarchy which had been implied by the librarian yesterday. Harker stood there shaking his head ever so slightly, the hint of a smile tugging at the corners of his mouth.

The one thing Ward could not stand was answering silly questions from "The Public", meaning anyone that had not the slightest inkling when it came to the 'metaphysical'. And he had also handled the vague insults from the previous day in classic Ward-fashion. As though he should ever have doubted his friend's astute mind.

* * *

As dusk was settling over the town of South Kensington, Harker came to the last page of the book.

He paused, knowing it was almost done, and a feeling of melancholy came upon him. As much as he looked forward to returning to his quiet happenings, he felt a connection with the spirit who, for however long now, had just wanted to finish reading the book. He found it difficult himself to leave anything undone, and wondered how many other spirits haunting the world could not leave the physical plane simply because they had unfinished business with a good novel.

"Everything alright?" Ward asked from across the room. He was shuffling a pile of newspapers, and it looked as though he were trying to put them back into some sort of order. "Yes," Harker replied. "Almost done here. What have you got?"

Ward smiled. "Proof that, for once, you are right, and I am . . . shall we say . . . not so correct?"

Harker chuckled. "Still cannot bring yourself to admit when you are wrong, can you?"

His friend shook his head. "Look, what's important is not only helping the spirit move on, but also to identify the who, just in case it has forgotten itself."

He leaned forward. "What have you found?"

"An English soldier by the name of Thomas King, who married a young Russian immigrant named Olga Aristov fifteen years ago. Three years after their marriage, he was killed in the Battle of Elandslaagte. Having no husband, she was forced to work the nearby fields, and died one evening walking home during a rather violent storm." He held up the discombobulated stack of newspapers. "I'm unsure as to which person you are reading to. It could be that she was reading it and translating to him, which could explain the book being closed when it was read in Russian . . ."

"Or it could be him. Perhaps he was trying to learn Russian."

They discussed it for a few moments, each of their thoughts drifting as they wondered at the possible history of the two unfortunate souls.

"Fortune does not always favor the living when it comes to war", Harker mused, falling silent. They both sat that way for a moment, pondering. The question as to which could be the ghost lent a morose finality to the proceedings. Lovers, taken from each other in their prime, before they even had a chance of making a family, let alone a life, together. Ward stared down at the jumbled papers, and Harker would have continued staring down at the book if it hadn't suddenly wiggled in his hands.

"Right, sorry," he said.

Then he finished reading the book to whomever was listening. As a compromise and a pleasant thought, he imagined that perhaps it was to the both of them.

* * *

They sat in silence for some time, staring at the book, which lay open to page two hundred and fifteen.

Ward reached across the table and flipped a few pages back. The librarian stared down at it in wonder. "You did it," he said, beaming with delight. "It's over with now? I can let this book out without someone bringing it back and complaining that it is broken?"

Harker absently pushed several pages aside, and the book remained still again, staying at whichever page he turned it to. "All done," he answered. "No more broken book."

"Well, gentlemen, I thank you both. It was getting rather difficult to explain this to fans of Dostoevsky. Not his most popular book, that would be *Crime and Punishment*, of course. But still, to read one author's book, you must read them all."

"You have a lot of those? Dostoevsky fans?" Ward stood and stretched the ache out of his bones. "One would not expect to find a large contingency of Russians this far inland."

"Oh, a whole section of town north of here is called 'Little Russia'. The wife and I go there for dinner at least twice a month."

Harker closed the book and held it out to the librarian. "Suppose we are all done here," he said, regret staining his voice. Standing in pause, he and Ward watched the librarian wander back into the stacks, *Demons* in hand.

"Listen, Jacob, I know this was successful, but why does it feel so . . ."

"Distressing?" Harker finished.

"Precisely. It is, quite possibly, the most depressing job we have completed."

Harker smiled at his friend. "It could be because we are looking at it as having been a job."

"If it wasn't a job," Ward, said, holding up the envelope with the ten pounds the librarian had just paid them, "then what was it, precisely?"

"I think that this time, it was more like . . ." Harker glanced around, grinning. "It was more like a favor. Like doing something nice for someone who can't thank you or repay your efforts."

Ward considered this for a moment, but then his eyes happened to catch a movement on the table. The table, which just a moment ago, had been empty, save for the empty pitcher and the two glasses.

"Uh . . . Jacob?"

"Yes?"

Harker was pulling on his topcoat. He glanced up at Ward and saw the look in his eyes. "What is it?"

Ward stood there pointing. Harker followed the direction of his finger and saw, sitting upon the table, right where *Demons* had sat not a minute before, a book twice the size of Dostoevsky's novel.

"Is that . . ." Harker began, but could not bring himself to finish, the words hanging in the air like an unfinished acknowledgment.

"I do believe that it is," Ward answered.

The men stared at each other, then at the oversized book, then back to each other.

Harker cleared his throat. "I do believe that this case can be left unsolved, yes?"

"Right," his friend answered. "Brandy tonight, or whiskey?"

"Both," Harker answered resolutely. They left as quickly as possible, not bothering to see the librarian on their way out.

And as their shadows slipped down the spiral staircase, Tolstoy's *War and Peace* flipped open to the first page.

MARY, VERIFIED

Mary Wiggins was at an impasse. The thirty-eight year old worked out of her large studio apartment near mid-city in Beacon Heights, doing medical billing.

The job was great—no commute, no boss breathing down her neck, no having to act friendly to people in the lunch room that she would never spend time with outside of the work environment. Just her, her cockatoo "Alex" (whom she called 'Alex' because that could be both a girls' or boys' name, and she had forgotten what gender the bird was when she bought it—she was positive the man at the shop had told her, but she couldn't quite recall by the time she got it home), her computer, and her rock collection.

Having gone to school for geology, there was not much call for the study of the earth's physical construct in a city, or even in the outlying area. So her degree was all but useless, except for on a personal level. She was the first child of four that had graduated college, and was not even the oldest. It was an accomplishment which she never verbalized to her siblings, but was one which crept into her brain on certain occasions. Say, for instance, her sister Claire was bragging about her job in the fashion industry (she was a saleswoman at a department store), her two children (one of whom was quite mean), and her husband Frank's job at some big company downtown (Frank was a moron). While she was glowing about her family and their myriad of victories, Mary would think to herself *yeah, but I have a degree!*, and it made listening to Claire that much easier.

Although she found that she never thought it whenever she was speaking to George, her younger brother. Not only did he have a degree—two to be exact—he was an attorney on Front St near the docks. Shady part of town, but he was able to actually use his degree. And while he would tell her about some of his cases, he never bragged, and he always asked her how she was, and usually remembered to ask about "Alex the Sexless Cockatoo", as he called her/him.

Her other brother, Bill, had been dead for eight years. He had been the oldest of the siblings, and had perished on a construction site when a wall caved in on him. She visited his grave at least once a month, telling him about current events in the world, anything amusing that Alex had said, and any interesting restaurants she had recently dined at. Unbeknownst to her, the information she provided at his gravesite made Bill one of the more knowledgeable and popular ghosts in the cemetery, as most of the other residents received news primarily of other relatives, or how inconvenient it was for them to have passed on and how could they have possibly thought to leave this relative a certain item in their will when said relation had absolutely no idea how to care for said item in the first place.

But Mary's current issue had nothing to do with any of her siblings, nor their ghosts. Her rent was being increased next month, which she would still be able to afford—but just barely. She began searching online for roommates, something she was loath to do, but could see no other option. If she wanted to continue to eat out twice a week and go to the movies a few times a month, not to mention maintaining her subscriptions to various geological magazines, she was going to need some help.

Sitting at her computer, she logged onto Greg's Stuff, a community website on which people posted things for sale, trade, or in some instances, free. Typically, "free" was referring to puppies or kittens, but the occasional sketchy sofa or ill-used dinnerware set were available at ABSOLUTELY NO COST TO YOU. It was also a place where people could find apartments for rent, and that was what brought Mary to the site that night. Anyone could peruse the website, but to post a listing, you had to create an account.

She made an account with her usual username and password (username 'maryrocks1974', password 'alexrocks2'), added her email address ('maryrockshard@mailer') and her cell phone number (don't be a creep, I'm not giving you her number), then waited while her request processed. It seemed to be taking some time, so she got up from her desk and refilled her tea.

When she returned to the computer there was a box in the middle of the screen which read "I am not a robot!" There was a smaller box next to this phrase, and Mary, a purveyor and explorer of the internet, knew exactly what it was. She moved the cursor and clicked on the checkmark, but just as she did so, the words changed to "I am not a serial killer!"

Her eyes got wide, but then giggled. Just last week she had been telling Bill's grave about how she was going to post a listing for a roommate, and had joked that she hoped she didn't get a serial killer responding to her ad. It was just her imagination playing tricks on her, like when you see a business sign really fast and misread it for something else. She had bought Alex at a pet store that at first glance had read "Erotic Pets"—but at a second, longer look, she had seen her error. "*Exotic* Pets" was the actual name of the store.

She waited while the hourglass on her computer spun around, sipping at her tea.

"Cage smells like poo!" Alex called from the other side of the room, his tone rather serious.

"It does not," Mary called back. "I just

cleaned it last weekend."

"Bad job, bad job," Alex responded.

The hourglass stopped spinning, and the expected columns of pictures came up. Typically, you clicked on the ones that were boats, or cats, or bathroom signs, but this time, something altogether different popped up.

There were four rows of five pictures which made up one complete image: a knife surrounded by blood. "Oh my goodness," Mary said.

"Language, dear!" Alex responded.

"Hush, bird," she said distractedly. She studied the screen, but could see no directions as to what she was supposed to be clicking on. The three blocks at the top, and the next two down on either side, were free from any part of the knife, or the giant splash of blood around it, so she clicked on those. At the last click of the mouse, the images faded away, and she waited while the hourglass spun around.

This time, a gun appeared right in the middle, taking up only the two middle squares. Leaning back in her chair, Mary studied the screen. There were no instructions at all—just a big white background, with the row of picture tiles in the middle. She minimized the website, opened up another one from her desk top, and perused online for a few moments. Nothing seemed the matter, so she maximized the window.

The same pictures greeted her.

Shaking her head, she opened another

internet connection and pulled up the Greg's Stuff site. She tried logging in, but got the 'invalid username and/or password' message. She closed that window and went back to the tiled picture.

Sighing, she closed it, then logged back on and went to the site again to start over. The same exact thing happened again—as soon as she clicked on the 'I am not a robot!' box, the words changed to 'I am not a serial killer!'. The picture with the knife came up again, and, seeing no other option, clicked on the same boxes again. She repeated the process when the picture of the gun came up again.

The image faded, and this time there was a picture of a bucket filled with blood, and a hand sticking out of the top of it. Mary put a hand to her mouth, shocked at the graphic visage. This was going too far—how would they even get a picture of such a thing? It was...

"*Offensive,*" she said.

She opened the site on another browser, went to the CONTACT US tab, and pulled up the customer service number. Dialing the number, she wondered at the audacity of the site. She had never had such a problem creating a login before, and there were a number of sites she was a member of. She had encountered the 'I am not a robot!' issue before, but usually after several moments of clicking on pictures of horses or ugly babies, she got into the sites just fine. Never had she encountered murder weapons and buckets of blood.

The phone rang twice, then an automated voice sounded in her ear, "Thank you for calling Greg's Stuff! For English, press one."

She pressed the one, rolling her eyes. How did they expect people that didn't speak English to continue on if they couldn't understand what they were hearing to begin with?

"For new accounts, press one. For existing accounts, press two."

She pressed the one, then waited as the phone clicked a few times. "For the Stuff For Sale department, press one. For the Stuff for Free department, press two. For our Personals page (the female voice said this line in a sexy manner, sounding like she was trying to get you all hot and bothered—which didn't work on Mary, by the way) for Hire, press four. For Customer Service, press five. To repeat this menu..."

Mary pressed the five. "Your call may be monitored for quality assurance purposes," she muttered. Then the voice repeated what Mary had said. She turned in her chair, eyeing Alex. He squawked at her, then said "Cage smells like poo."

"Oh you smell like poo, you dirty bird," she replied.

"I'm sorry?" said a male voice on the phone.

Mary sat up straight in her chair. "Oh, no, not you, sorry, I was talking to my bird."

There was a pause, then the voice said, "Okay, well, how can I help you today?"

She shook her head at the bird, then turned

back to the computer. "I'm having a problem creating an account," she said. "I can't get past the part where you verify that you aren't a serial kil—I mean, the 'not a robot' part." She could feel herself blushing, which made her feel ridiculous, as the customer service rep wasn't someone she would probably ever speak to again. Why should she care what he thought?

"You mean the verification page?"

"Yes, that's the one."

"I apologize, ma'am, but Greg's Stuff does not run that site. You would need to contact them about any issues with the verification process."

"But there's no number on the screen, just this picture of a bucket. And it's offensive."

There was a pause on the other end. Then the man cleared his throat, and said "A picture of an offensive bucket?"

She rolled her eyes again. "It isn't the bucket that's offensive, it is what is *inside* of the bucket that I'm having issues with."

"Well, is it, like, click all the squares with the bucket until there are no buckets left kind of thing?"

"I'm not clicking on the bucket—I told you, it's offensive. Not the bucket, but what's in it."

Another pause, then he suggested she try clicking on the parts of the bucket that weren't offensive. It sounded to her like he was smiling when he said it.

"There aren't any squares to click on that

don't have the bucket in it."

"Is it like a 'two girls and a cup' picture? Two girls and a bucket?" the man asked.

"I'm sure I don't know what that is," Mary responded, although the righteousness in her voice said otherwise.

"Right," the man answered. "I apologize, ma'am, but you would have to finish the process in order to register. Unless you can click the bucket, I'm afraid you are at an impasse."

"Well, if you could see the bucket, you wouldn't want to click on it, either."

"What's in the bucket, ma'am?"

"I'd rather not say."

"Is it gross?"

"And offensive," she replied.

She hung up the phone then, her eyes never leaving the image. After a moment's thought, she moved the cursor to the hand sticking out of the bucket. It seemed almost as if it were trying to escape the bloody contents of its cage, and was the only part of the picture that did not contain the rim of the bucket.

Mary clicked on the hand, and the image slowly dissolved.

The screen stayed that way for what seemed like five minutes—just a cold, off-white nothing. She could see an image faintly in the monitor, a woman, staring blankly back at her. It was the desk lamp; it cast a ghostly reflection of her, and she looked like an entirely different person. She reached out and switched the lamp off, negating the disturbing reflection on her screen.

Then a new box showed up in the middle of the browser.

"I am a serial killer!" it read, with a little box next to it to click on.

"Oh, donkey balls," she said, opening another browser.

"Donkey balls!" Alex exclaimed.

"Precisely," Mary muttered, and began hunting Google for the customer service number of the stupid verification company. It took her twenty minutes of digging through customer responses, complaints, testimonies, business opportunities, and ways around it so she could watch porn more easily. Not really what she was looking for, so she thought about it for a moment, then typed in "I am not a serial killer verification".

At first, all she saw were ads for a movie that had most of those words in its title. A few pages in, though, and she found it. Someone else had had the same issue. She clicked on the link, and it brought up a complaint with one of those local sites that supposedly monitored such things. She read the entire message, and at the very end, she found the phone number for the company.

Just in case it wasn't some random number the guy had made up or, even worse, his own number, she ran it through Google, and saw that it did indeed go to the verification company. She dialed the number on her cell, then closed out the browser and brought up the cheery screen that wanted her to click on the box saying that she was, indeed a serial killer.

The phone rang a few times in her ear, then a recorded voice came on the line. "Thank you for calling The Image Capture Verification Company, the World's Premiere Service in internet verification."

She rolled her eyes again—they were getting quite the workout that night—and waited for the lady to list off the options.

"Please press one for English," the voice said. Mary pushed the button.

The menu cycled, and the next option came up. "For businesses wishing to utilize our patented Verification Process, press one. If you are interested in franchise opportunities, press two." Mary raised her eyebrows at that last one, but before she could even consider the option, the menu continued.

"If you have encountered a problem during our patented Verification Process, press three." Mary smiled, and pressed the three. Now she was getting somewhere.

"If you are a robot, please press one."

And now this was getting ridiculous. She stared down at her phone, as if to check and make sure it hadn't been replaced with some sort of trick phone. "If you are not a robot, press two."

She mashed the two down angrily. Would

a Spanish speaking robot have been able to locate their number? She doubted it, and the entire process was beginning to really tick her off. Which is surprising, because the last time Mary was really ticked off had been in 2003, the day her high school sweetheart "Sam" had broken up with her —which was also the same day her sister Claire had notified her via wedding invitation that she was marrying "Frank", a man she had known for all of four months. Mary and Sam had been dating for eight years, and never once had the topic of marriage come up. So, yes, she was quite incensed that day. Now the anger was bubbling up again.

"If you are a serial killer, please press one."

Mary stared at the accusing lie on her computer, and waited for the next option. Only the next option never came; it simply repeated the first one: "if you are a serial killer, please press one."

She looked down at her phone, then pushed the button marked 'two'. Just in case.

"I'm sorry, that is not an option. If you are serial killer, please press one."

She pressed the zero to see if that would get her to a live person—it didn't. "I'm sorry, that is not an option. If you are a serial killer, please press one."

"Mother FUGGER!" Mary screamed into the phone.

"Donkey balls!" Alex replied.

Mary shot the bird a warning glance, and it

promptly hit its head under its wing. She glared at the phone, said "Mother fuggit", and pressed the one button. There was a brief silence, then: "Hold for the next available agent."

Then she heard Barry Manilow in her ear. Instead of having a soothing effect, Barry was ticking her off even more. Mandy was a slut, and left poor Barry. Even though Barry was gay. Unless it was a guy named "Mandy"—that could have other repercussions. Mary began to really listen to the lyrics to see if it was possible for Mandy to be a guy, and then began getting mad at herself for allowing the oldest trick in the book to have the desired, soothing effect on her.

"Mandy" ended, and in walked Neil Diamond. Neil was only marginally better than Barry; the selection was "I Am, I Said", which, while not her favorite, had a desperate yet slightly uplifting quality to the chorus...

Mary pounded the top of her desk in frustration, her fist stinging sharply from the impact. The "make the angry lady complacent" bit was pushing her over the edge. The last time she had ever punched anything was in fourth grade when Warren Dufrain had tried kissing her, and that hadn't hurt at all that she could remember —although the shot had bloodied Warren's nose, it having been the largest target on his face. She fought against the music, gritting her teeth and silently resolving to give whomever answered a piece of her mind. She stared at her screen and that horrible accusation during the entire song.

"We apologize for the delay," the recorded voice told her once the song was over. "All of our representatives are currently assisting other killers. Please continue to hold, and your call will be answered in the order it was received."

"Should've pushed two for Spanish, would have gotten through quicker," Mary said, her voice filled with reproach.

"That option would have taken even longer, as we currently do not employ a Spanish speaking representative. Please continue to hold."

Mary took the phone away from her face and stared at it. The voice was the same recorded one she had heard during the entire call, yet it had just spoken back to her.

"Hello?" she asked, and was immediately answered by "hello darkness my old friend"—Simon and Garfunkel, wouldn't you know—and had to stop herself from throwing her phone across the room. It wasn't that she didn't like the song, she did; but right now, she didn't want the freaking sound of silence she wanted—

"—a mother freaking OPERATOR!"

She screamed the last word into the phone, her hand clutching the phone in a grip which made the plastic on the phone shift. She relaxed her fist by the tiniest of margins, allowing the phone to continue its purpose in life for the time being.

Before the song could reach its end, there

came a click on the line, and then an Indian man said, "this is Pee-ter, how can I be of assisting today?"

Staring intently at her monitor, and speaking through her clenched jaw, Mary replied with "You have got to be kidding me."

There was a moment of silence, then the man said, "I am sorry ma'am, but this is Pee-ter, and I am here to help you."

She closed her eyes, trying to settle herself down.

"Peter, are you in America, or in another country?"

"While I am not allowed to give out my exact location, I am happy to tell you that we are in Witchy-taw, Kansas. How can I be assisting you today?"

She sighed, but held her anger in check. It would not benefit her to let loose on Pee-ter, as they probably had guidelines for angry customers, which could include hanging up the phone. And Mary was not about to have to call back and go through all of that again.

"Peter. I cannot seem to get past this screen which keeps telling me that I am a serial killer."

"Okay, I think I see the problem," Pee-ter responded.

"No, I don't think you do, unless this is a glitch other people have encountered."

"No ma'am, it is no glitch."

"Well, Peter, I clicked on the boxes, and

there were murder weapons and a bucket of blood on my computer screen. I found it all…" She swallowed, and mentally rolled the word around in her mouth. "…*offensive*."

"I see, and I do think I am knowing the problem here, ma'am."

"Please, do tell." Mary tapped her fingers on the desk, sure that whatever Middle Eastern country "Peter" was really in, they probably didn't have much issues with online verification, let alone serial killers.

"Was the first screen a knife?" he asked her.

"Yes," she answered. "Yes it was."

"And did you frame the knife and the gun?"

She narrowed her eyes for a moment, thinking. "By 'frame', do you mean did I click on the squares all around the outside?"

"Yes ma'am. Like a frame around the weapons."

"Like a wall frame that you put a picture in?" she asked. "I can assure you I wasn't trying to draw attention to the weapons—"

"Yes, okay. And the picture with the bucket —"

"Oh, now that was the worst one," she said.

"Yes, okay. The bucket; did you click on the hand, or on the squares with the bucket?"

She wondered where he was going with all of this. It didn't sound like a computer issue, not with the questions he was asking. Unless, of course, it was some magical combination that created the error.

"I clicked on the hand," she said.

"Yes, okay. I know exactly what the problem is, ma'am."

"Oh, thank goodness," she replied. "I thought there was a problem here—"

"You are in denial, ma'am."

"—with your programing...wait, what?" She stared down at the phone incredulously.

"You are a serial killer, ma'am."

Now she stared at the phone, her mouth hanging open, her eyes wide.

"Hello, ma'am, are you there?"

"Is this a joke?" she asked.

"No ma'am."

She could detect no amusement in his voice, just the same deadpan delivery he'd displayed throughout the call. It sounded as though he was reading from a script, which he more than likely was.

"What—and I want you to be exact here, Pee-*ter*—what precisely makes you think that I am a serial killer?"

"Algorithms, ma'am."

"Algorithms."

"Yes ma'am. Algorithms. They do not lie."

"How..."

"You see," Peter said, "when you clicked on the squares around the weapons, that indicates a desire to see the weapons unhindered. Also, if you look at the weapons for a long time, that indicates a desire to use them, or a history with them. And you click on the hand, the result of using such weapons. Mathematically, those choices, and the amount of time it took you to click, indicate that you are a serial killer ma'am.

"Is there anything else I can be assisting with today?"

Mary had nothing. It took a moment for her brain to process this approach to her choices, and when she realized fully what he was saying, she became desperate to prove her innocence.

"Ma'am?"

"No, no, that isn't right. It took me a long time to click because I didn't know what to do!'

There was a pause ("Peter" was looking up the appropriate response in his script), then he said, "You were admiring the weapons and what they stood for."

She felt as though she had been slapped. "You are out of your ever-loving mind, Pedro," she said.

"My name is Pee-ter, ma'am. Pedro is off today."

"Listen up, Johnny Five, I'm done with being insulted. I want your supervisor."

"Certainly. If you hold on for just a moment, I will connect you."

She heard a click, and then the soothing sounds of Air Supply began oozing from her phone. "Donkey tits!" she yelled at the phone.

"Balls!" Alex offered, then ducked his head

back under his wing.

Thankfully, before Air Supply could fully explain to her just why they were all out of love (really, the lyrics..."tormented and torn apart"'...), there was a click, and another Indian voice was on the line.

"This is Chad the Supervisor, how may I be helping you today?"

Mary sighed. "Chad? Really? Do you guys get assigned a different name every day, or do you pull them out of a hat?"

"Umm...this is Chad every day?"

"Listen, Chad, because I'm at the end of my rope here..."

"You are the young lady that keeps getting the serial killing verification, yes?"

She hesitated. "Essentially, yes."

"Okay, I think I am knowing the problem," Chad said.

"Is this another algorithm issue, Chad? Because that's what Peter told me, and I'm not believing it for a minute."

"Oh, no," he answered, laughing. "Is most definitely not a problem with any silly algorithm, ma'am."

"Thank goodness," Mary said, smiling for the first time in what felt like months. "I was starting to think someone was pranking me."

"No ma'am, no pranking today."

"Great. So can you help me with this?"

"Most definitely. The problem is that you

are in denial ma'am. As soon as you accept that you are a serial killer, there will no longer be a problem."

Mary stared at the phone, fully expecting it to explode or disappear altogether. Either that phone number she had found was a complete hoax, or...well, she really didn't want to think of the other alternative.

"Okay, you guys have had your fun," she said.

"No joking here today, ma'am. We take our job very seriously."

"Uh-huh. Listen, what town are you in?"

There was a brief pause, then Chad came back with "While I am not allowed to give out my exact location, I am happy to tell you that we are in Witching-taw, Kansas."

"It's Wichita!" she yelled. "Did they teach you how to properly pronounce English when they made you memorize the freaking script?!"

Chad was silent for a moment, and when he did speak again, he sounded genuinely offended. "I am sorry for any issues you may be encountering, ma'am, but Peter and I have been trying to assist you to the best of our abilities. Is no reason for you to be getting personal about our speaking abilities. And referring to Pee-ter as 'Johnny Five' is an outdated but still offensive stereotype. *Ma'am.*"

Mary closed her eyes and pinched the bridge of her nose. "Look...I'm sorry, *Chad.* I'm normally not like this. I swear to you I am not a racist. I'm just frustrated. And a little on edge."

"I understand, ma'am."

"You do?"

"Of course," he said. "You are not the first serial killer I have ever spoken to, and you people can be very intense."

She stared at the phone.

"And at this point, the only thing left for you to do is just push on the button," Chad said, quite cheerfully. "Just click on that box, everything will be better."

Mary looked at the computer monitor, at that little box.

"Go ahead. What are you concerned about, it is just a little box." Now Chad's voice had a taunting quality to it, like he was daring her.

"Besides, clicking on the box, does that make things real?"

She tilted her head, pinning the phone between her ear and her shoulder. Then she moved the cursor over to the box.

"Clicking on a computer screen never hurt anyone before, did it?" Chad asked. "Why should this time be any different?"

"Because," Mary said, and even to her, her voice sounded like it was full of doubt, "because I'm not a serial killer."

Her finger hovered over that left mouse button, trembling slightly. She was actually scared to push it, and Chad was right—what would it really hurt, to click on that button?

"Are you sure about that, ma'am? Just because you never killed anyone does not mean you are not a serial killer. You shouldn't doubt yourself. My mother always told me, 'Chad,' she would say, 'you shouldn't be doubting yourself.' If she was on the phone now, she would tell you the same thing, ma'am. Stop doubting, and just do."

Mary watched her finger descend until it hit the button on the mouse. Then she looked up at the screen as the checkmark appeared next to the words "I am a serial killer".

"Did you push the button, ma'am?"

"Oh, yes," she answered.

"There," Chad said. "That wasn't so hard a thing to do now, was it?"

Mary stared at the monitor, watching the box slowly dissolve, and said, "I'll let you know after I find a roommate."

THE EVIL END

Priest looked Deacon in his one good eye and said, in all seriousness, "It's the ass-end of the alphabet. That's where all the trouble's at, mate."

Deacon stared at his companion, trying to decide if he was having a rare bout of seriousness or not. A quick study of the other's features told him nothing--there was always a twinkle in Priest's eyes, always a smile playing at the corners of his mouth, always a slight blush to his pale cheeks. Even the tone of his English accent could not be relied upon as a dead giveaway. He looked and sounded as serious about this topic as he had been about running naked through the Saint Theresa Convent in Iowa every forty-two years, and as serious as his idea centuries ago of starting that plague in old Europe.

"Think about it, then," he said, leaning back in the seat. "Vampires, Werewolves, and Zombies--all at the ass-end of the bleedin' alphabet."

Deacon shifted, trying to get comfortable, knowing he could not. Church pews were built for pain, but the irony of the two of them being in an actual church was worth the discomfort. It just always amazed him that humans would come to a place of worship and not have a cushion to sit on. Like having a sore ass was proper penance for anything, or being uncomfortable for an hour showed how penitent one was.

Priest, as always, looked completely at home on the hard, wooden bench. His black trench coat was opened about him, spread like the wings of a great bat as he rested his arms along the length of the pew. His long legs disappeared under the bench in front of him. Even his pale, bony, angular face looked at ease--all the exact opposite of Deacon, who now balanced on the points of his toes—much more pleasant on the ass, this position was—crouched in the pew, a tense, dark spring ready to uncoil in a flash of agitated violence.

He was shorter and stockier than Priest--the exact opposite physically. It was their differences that made them such great partners. They had outlasted every other duo on the planet, and were a model of cooperation and grace, two elements that blended well and hardly ever fought.

"What about Poltergeists?" Deacon asked. "The P's are about two-thirds of the way through, not at the end. Those are a bit on the nasty side."

Priest smiled, as if he had already anticipated his partner's every possible response, which was probably exactly what he had done; Deacon knew that he rarely said anything, serious or not, without having first thought it out for a decade or so. "Small time. Ye could say that's where the alphabet starts to go rotten. I mean, the whole bloody thing is bad. Just gets progressively worse."

Deacon thought this over for a moment. He stared down at the floor, where countless humans had tread previously, all to worship, beg forgiveness, and expound upon the sins of others. He knew Priest was awaiting his response, and he smiled as one came to him.

"So, if it starts off bad, and since everything bad progresses from the start of humans and everything thereafter is evil in the image of humans, how is the beginning so much different than the end? If it starts with humans in their natural state, and ends with them in a dead or undead state, what does it matter where you start?"

Priest shook his head, himself smiling. "That's where yer wrong."

"How so? Evil is inherently human. No other animal expresses that trait. The alphabet starts bad and ends bad, too."

"The entire alphabet may be based on the 'uman experience, but it starts out with Arseholes and Bitches."

Deacon laughed. "Show me a Zombie that isn't an Asshole--"

"--and I'll show ye a Zombie what's a Bitch," Priest finished. "Can only have one or th' other. Now, in between is where the proof lies, ennit?"

He stood and stretched, his bones and muscles aching. "Hate these frigging pews," he said. "I still think 'umans made 'em this way to bleedin' punish themselves."

Deacon eyed him suspiciously. "I thought you liked the pews. You never complained about them before."

Priest smiled. "I like the confessionals. Those are comfy and dark. But there's something about being out in the open 'ere, in all the light...."

As Priest's voice trailed off and his gaze wandered over the opulence that was the interior of the Catholic Church of Beacon Heights, Deacon silently marveled at his friend's ability to always keep him guessing. He always thought he knew how the other's unpredictability worked, but inevitably it left him shaking his head. A marriage of thousands of years, and never a dull moment.

"Enyways," Priest said, suddenly snapping back to his topic of the evening, "let's progress to Ghosts."

"Aren't you skipping a few of the obvious ones?" Deacon asked, his eyebrows raised.

"*Because* they are obvious, mate. Now, Ghosts are what? The souls of dead 'umans. Not a big deal, as there isn't much they can actually do. They are neither good nor bad. They just are. What they were as 'umans doesn't matter so much; they're simply stuck here."

"Ghouls?"

"Angry Ghosts—follow 'Ghosts' alphabetically, don't they?"

"Harpies?"

"Bad rap. Remember Stella, that Harpy from Wales? Nice lady, that."

"Oh, yeah, she made a good tea, didn't she?"

Priest nodded. "And I know what yer next guess is: Lycanthropes. Nothing more than a trained Werewolf, ennit? Most of 'em vegetarians. Still not that bad. And since most Lycanthropes consider themselves cursed, yet still can control the freakin' change...in my book, they're a bunch of pansies."

"Are Mummies next?"

Priest smiled. "They shouldn't even make the list. You'd have to be legless and blind for a Mummy to catch you. But, yes, they make the list. They are dead 'umans in the flesh, so they have to be on the list. Now come the Poltergeists. Nasty little boogers, but not the worst."

"Pissed-off Ghosts."

"Precisely. And, harder to get rid of."

Deacon stood, stretching his own legs. "Pissed-off and *stubborn* Ghosts."

"Then there's the Vampires--blood suckers, every one. Aim for arteries, and make a big bloody mess. You ever see a Vamp use a napkin? They play with the idea of love, but they're more like rock stars. They're in it fer the drugs and the groupies."

Deacon shook his head. "Vampires can't get it up. How could they be in it for the sex?"

"Who said anything about sex?" Priest answered.

"You said 'groupies'. Groupies means sex. You remember those groupies Jagger gave us back in '73? Sex? Drugs? Rock and roll...."

Priest looked his friend in his one eye, considering. "Okay," he finally responded. "I'll give ye that one. But what about Werewolves? They eat, kill for fun, and they make an even *bigger* mess. At least Vampires try to hide their prey. Wolves leave the carcasses right out in the open. No class at all. And, they hump like rabid rabbits.

"But Zombies? They aren't picky. And they don't even stop when they get full. They'll eat a 'uman straight through, and stop to vomit a dozen times before they're done, just so's they can go back and *eat some more*! They don't bother cleaning up afterwards, they don't hide, they don't sleep, they don't mate, all they bloody do is eat. Totally non-productive members of society. Zombies are, essentially, the ultimate Assholes."

Deacon smiled. "You forgot Witches."

Priest shook his head. "Most of 'em are bad."

"But we knew a lot of good ones back in the day."

"Oh, of course we did. That's why we started the plague, remember? To stop all those idiots from burning 'em."

"The first time, yeah," Deacon replied. "But all the other times they were persecuting them? Remember Salem?"

"Oh, well, they weren't even Witches, then, were they? 'Wiccans', they like to call themselves now. Just another religion, and a whole other alphabet. Except for Christians. Them, we have to include in *this* Alphabet."

"Because the word 'Christian' includes most religions?"

"For the true definition of the word, it includes *all* religions, and is part of the human condition, evil or not."

"Right after Bitches."

Now Priest smiled. "Precisely. Arseholes. Bitches. Christians."

"It's almost midnight," Deacon said, shaking his head, but smiling.

"Ah, good. Time for the exclamation point o' the evening."

Together they walked down a side aisle, heading to the front of the church. "As far as Witches go, they were mostly bad back then. A few good ones, but a few of every type of monster tried to be good at some point in time, didn't they? Except for the Zombies. No morality to them. Nasty bastards."

"What about Satanists?"

Priest chuckled. "Should classify 'em under 'losers', as in 'I can't get laid so let's start a club and kill some goats and slip all the girls a mickey'. Bunch of tossers. They'd 'ave to go on our religious alphabet, anyways."

In the distance, they heard the muffled peals of a bell ringing. As they drew even with the first pew, they saw the outline of a Ghost begin to form before them. "Right on time," Deacon said.

They watched the Ghost materialize; it was like watching a glass bottle fill with smoke, becoming more and more solid, but still having that hazy look to it. Features became more defined as the "smoke" solidified. First it was vaguely human, and then they could see it was a man. Then they could tell that the man wore the clothes of the priesthood, and as the final details became defined, they could see the dark hair color.

Priest shook his head. "Ghosts. Not much to 'em, just the soul latching on to a location 'cause of mem'ries. This one, he was a real Arsehole."

The Ghost turned to them, an expression of shock on its face. "You can see me?"

"Ooo, a Ghost that knows it's dead. This one's a borderline Poltergeist, ennit," Deacon said, rubbing his big hands together.

"Of course we can see you," Priest answered. "We know all about you, 'Father Gene'. Church was second in your soul, right after little boys."

The Ghost looked away, then back at them, defiantly. "You can prove nothing, none of them could."

"Oh, save it, ye daft prick. Do we look like coppers? Besides, you're dead. Do ye really think we have to *prove* anything?"

Deacon stepped forward. "There is a special place for you, where we are taking you. Have you ever read Dante?"

The Ghost shook its head, looking down in concern at the hand that now gripped its forearm, then back up at the eye patch on the short, dark man that held him. "How can you touch me? Are you dead, too?"

Deacon groaned, ignoring the question. "How does a man of the cloth not read Alighieri? What is this world coming to?"

"Too bad," Priest said. "'E had most of it right. If you had read it, ye probably would have learned how to do that nasty stuff by yerself, and not with the altar boys. Would have saved yerself an eternity of...well, you'll see."

Deacon lifted the Ghost over his head with one hand. Father Gene found he could not move, and cried out plaintively at his sudden paralysis. He was like a stuffed toy in the hands of the other, who acted as if he weighed about the same as one, too. "Dante never really said specifically which circle pedophiles went to, but in case you were wondering, it's the eighth. Sandwiched between a few of the Bolgias."

The Ghost stared at him, clueless. "Nothing?" He looked over at Priest, who merely shrugged. "They have to learn Latin in school, don't they? And they don't have to read any Dante?" He looked back up at the priest. "Not even *Paradiso*? No?

"Okay, then. Let's just get on with it. You're probably wondering who we are, aren't you?"

Priest smiled. "This is me favorite part," he said, as he walked into the Ghost's field of vision. "We've come to take you 'ome. To Hell."

They could see the revelation of it all come slowly into the eyes of the Ghost-Poltergeist, like how it had slowly materialized in front of them not a few moments before. "Ah, now 'e gets it."

"So do I," Deacon said, a broad smile expanding over his face, revealing needle-like teeth in what was stretching into a gaping pit of a mouth. "Us. The D's. Demons."

Priest nodded, grinning himself.

"Demons. We come between Christians and Evil."

There was a moment of silence, then they both laughed. The volume of their laughter deepened as it came out, their voices changing as their bodies stretched and pulled against the gravity that before had crushed them down to human size.

Their true forms began to expand outward, encompassing the Ghost of the pedophile priest, filling the entire front end of the church. "That's rich," one of them said. "I didn't know whether you were joking or not."

"How often am I serious?" said the other.

The priest's voice was barely audible. "Wait," he said. "I don't get it."

There was a loud cracking sound as the church was suddenly empty and air rushed in to fill the void left by the Demons and their charge. The ensuing wind, albeit a brief one, was enough to extinguish every candle in the church. Following the darkness was the silence, which fell over the hardened pews like a heavy blanket.

For a few moments, the church was empty of everything but the night and the quiet.

Then:

"Did you hear that, Gabe?" a voice from the rafters asked. Its timbre was soft, its tone almost musical in nature.

"Yeah. 'A' is for 'Assholes'," came the reply from the upper balcony.

"Bunch of disrespectful gits. Everyone knows 'A' is for 'Angels'."

THE GREAT OFFICE MELEE OF 1978

-or-

LOVE AND LUST AT THE OFFICE

There was a part of the day, every day, when Leon Burkett paused, looked out a window, and got the blankest of expressions upon his face.

It usually happened around one-thirty, precisely an hour after he had finished lunch, and it was something which happened seemingly on a primal level. He was not conscious of doing it; he never noticed the time and thought "oh, I need to look out the window for a moment". He did not have a feeling of anticipation or anxiety or confusion. It was simply a moment of blankness, as though his mind were resetting itself.

There was no actual re-booting going on; it was, to his mind and body, a pause.

If he took his lunch earlier than the usual

time, his moment of pause happened earlier as well. If he was late, so was the empty gaze out the window. Hardly anyone ever noticed it; working in a corner desk for several years bought oneself a certain amount of anonymity. People tended to notice you less when you were a usual part of the scenery, which Leon most definitely was. He had worked for the same company for nearly ten years, which was saying a lot for an employer whose open-door policy operated on a motorized ejection seat.

The fact that he had survived for that long in a cut-throat environment was not anything he ever received any recognition for, however. At two years, he had been presented with a dress shirt with the company logo emblazoned on the chest. When he hit his fifth anniversary, he was awarded a personalized pen—which also had the company logo on it.

At ten years, he was due to get a wood-encased clock. He had seen the award presented twice before at the company retreat, and the clock, while nice in its factory-made glossy presentation, had the company letters burnt into the back that the little pendulum swung in front of. When he had first seen it, he had wondered if it could hypnotize or brainwash you if you stared at it for too long. Not that that would surprise anyone—everything the company gave you had its name proudly carved etched, printed, or summarily burnt into it. From coffee cups to insulated mugs, there apparently was no shortage of items with the words "Percy", "Montgomery", and "Cash" stitched or permanently marked upon them. The firm was a big believer in self-promotion, even with the employees that already worked there.

On Thursday, January the fourth, lunch was the same as usual: a tuna fish on rye, light mayo, minced onions, and Romaine lettuce. He also had the same sides: eight baby carrots, one piece of celery cut into three sections, and a few pieces of cauliflower. No dressing.

While he ate his lunch, he read a western novel (the title of which is not all that important, due to the fact that Leon Burkett is not going to be with us much longer), of which he folded the top corners of the page down whenever he was not reading. When he was reading, if a line or passage struck him as interesting, he took out a pen, circled the area of the page he wished to revisit, and would then fold up the bottom corner of the page.

In case you had not caught on yet, by the earlier mention of his fondness for onions (which are evil) and cauliflower without dressing (which is gross), not to mention his penchant for destroying books, Leon Burkett really was not someone you should care about it. This isn't his story anyway, so don't feel bad when he dies. (It's coming soon, don't fret—he is certainly not a character you fret over.)

* * *

So on that cold, overcast day in January of 1978, after his usual lunch adorned with the Devil's fruit (minced) and a particularly enthusiastic reading and underlying of an unnamed Western novel, Leon looked up as he always did.

Only this time, there was a tiny cactus in the window. His eyes immediately locked onto the cactus; he frowned, as the tiny green plant had not been there yesterday, and the window, which was a tiny square set at head-level on an otherwise white and featureless wall, now offered an obstructed view. He immediately stood and gazed over the desks to give the cactus owner a piece of his mind.

He paused, but it was not his usual pause—oh, no. This was a pause borne of confusion. The other pause, the regular one, was a mindless sort of thing. This was a dead-on, terribly perplexed pause.

Somewhere deep inside of Leon, whether on his subconscious level or somewhere more primal and basic, there was the knowledge that that particular day's pause had been missed. As it had been a regular event in his existence, the missed pause had (for Leon) dire consequences.

His finger half raised, his mouth half-open to voice his complaint, and with one of his eyebrows pointed at an obvious upwards slant, Leon Burkett felt something tiny pop in his brain, and he promptly fell face forward on his desk. Dead. (Told you it was coming soon.)

Three hours after his body was removed from the property, the office staff pilfered the supplies from his desk.

The cactus belonged to one Agnes Fisk, who worked data entry.

To compensate for a dramatic loss of revenue—which could possibly be in part due to how much the company spent on pens and stress balls and coffee mugs with their logo imprinted upon them—the company had moved half of the data entry staff up to the third floor. The other half were given parking validations, one week's severance pay, and a Percy, Montgomery, and Cash tote bag (leftover from the retreat in 1974, in which the spelling for 'Percy' was incorrect) to carry all of their personal effects home in.

The invasion of the data entry clerks was the subject of much speculation in the break room when there were no data entry people present. Everyone was complaining about the loss of personal space, the seemingly smaller desks, and, by God, the overwhelming noise those people brought with them. As they never had to speak to customers, the endless prattle was an inane litany of whose cat had done what, opinions on the latest episode of "Three's Company", upcoming vacation plans (which no one ever really took, as the managers all frowned upon vacation requests), and how sexy Burt Reynolds was. It drove the other departments mad; as there was no empty area on the third floor, the wayward data entry clerks had been placed wherever an empty desk—or the space to fit one from the abolished second floor—could be fit.

The integration was not going well. Lunches had begun to disappear from the middle fridge in the breakroom, and this was, as you can imagine, blamed upon the infiltrators. Not a day went by that found an angry sales rep stalking the floor, looking for the thief of his or her sandwich. The situation was growing volatile, and the seemingly untimely death—well warranted or not—of one Leon Burkett did nothing to ease the situation.

Agnes's desk was one row over from Leon's, facing the tiny window in the plain boring wall. The cactus had been on her desk downstairs for four months and had been a gift from her ex-boyfriend. There had barely been enough room on her desk for the tiny potted plant, with the computer taking up most of the space. Yet it (and her computer, unfortunately) had survived the trek up to hostile territory in December the previous year. It was not until that fateful day in January, however, that she thought to place it in the window.

Agnes's motivation was simple: cacti persevered in the desert, an environment which was under constant sunlight. Therefore, her little cactus, if it wanted to grow up big and majestic and dangerously pointy like its peers, needed sunlight. Thus, the window.

* * *

Leon was loved quietly and afar by Jean Cline, a stout woman in her mid-forties who had never had the pleasure of a man's company. Well, she did have one liaison in 1957, but it hadn't been pleasurable in the least.

Her adoration and rather questionable fixation on a man who enjoyed minced onions and defacing perfectly good books is not what we should focus on, however; she accepted all of Leon's flaws (obviously no matter how heinous—I imagine that if he spent his spare time punting babies and chucking puppies as if they were javelins she still would have been madly in love with him) without question. Except for the inexcusable flaw of him being married.

For that, she did not entirely blame the man (a word I use loosely). Rather, she imagined him to be married to an evil, vile woman, one who had trapped him in a loveless marriage and spent all of his money on shoes and sporty cars and tennis lessons from some dark-skinned boy with a large...well, you get the picture. Anything which anyone would see as a flaw in Leon's person or character was written off by Jean as someone else's fault.

When she was home, reading romance novels aloud to her four cats—except for the steamy parts when someone lost a button or an entire shirt, as she did not want to have to explain human copulation to a bunch of animals that rutted whenever the moon was full or one of them seemed particularly angry—she likened her and Leon as the main characters. Sometimes, she would even cross out the names of the characters and replace them with 'Jean' and 'Leon'.

Apparently, she had the same respect for books that the object of her silent affections did. And that is how she stayed—silent. To voice her love to a man married, a man who seemed to not even be aware of her existence, would have been far too scandalous for the workplace. It was too professional of an environment for her to imagine Leon as anything other than a coworker. Or the newly hired farmhand in "Hay and Roses" that swept the plantation owner's daughter off of her feet and carried her up to the hayloft on a rainy afternoon.

So while her adoration for Leon Burkett remained an unspoken and ultimately unfulfilled desire of the heart, her hatred for Agnes Fisk was something she was having difficulty controlling.

* * *

By Valentine's Day, Jean Cline could remain silent no longer.

She had seen Agnes place the cactus on the little window sill. She had seen her not-lover's reaction to the placement of said plant. She had seen him rise from his seat, then fall over dead upon his electric typewriter, his lifeless hand knocking the phone from the receiver, which had swung by its short cord above the hideous carpet before Chad from Accounting could no longer stand the noise of the un-dialed phone any longer and had replaced it by inhumanely moving Leon's dead limb aside with Leon's stapler (which was later pilfered by Rose Layman from data entry, who had lost hers in the move up from the second floor).

Jean had seen it all, knew who had been responsible for the demise of her 'Carlo' (from "Latin Love of the Western Prairies", in which she had managed to replace their names in all of the sexy parts), and knew by name and face every person that had disrespected him by stealing all of the good supplies before she could get any herself. She had just wanted something to remember him by as she silently mourned his loss, and all that had been left after the office vultures had descended was three loose paperclips and one row of staples.

Jean was plenty angry, and the flower delivery to the desk of one Agnes 'She of the Deadly Cactus' Fisk was the last straw.

* * *

Unbeknownst to Agnes, her ex-boyfriend Leonard was having difficulty replacing her with someone else that would allow him to slap uglies with them.

In a desperate attempt to win her back—at least for the weekend, long enough for him to release a month and a half's worth of pent up sexual energy—he had ordered six roses from Ballard's Bulbs and Such on Fifth Avenue. Because really, a dozen was too much, and sent the wrong message entirely. He didn't love her, so much as he wanted to love *on* her.

Agnes was unaware of the single-minded direction of Leonard's "thoughts", and totally fell for his trickery. After all, she had been keeping the two-inch tall cactus (which reminded her of her ex-boyfriend's naughty bits—short, fat, covered in tiny squiggles) in the best health possible as far as her knowledge of caring for cacti was concerned. Upon receipt of the half-dozen roses nestled amongst an explosion of Baby's Breath (which reminded her of the patch of hair located just above his rather sad penis—abundant, overgrown, and oddly white on the ends), her heart fluttered—honestly, not her heart, but too much more description might place this tale in another category altogether, and it might have to be renamed “Office Heat in Wintertime”—and a feeling of compassion and love overcame her.

Such a powerful feeling it was that she knew, deep down, that the roses and the cactus must be placed in close proximity of each other. They were both symbols of his undying yet sporadic affections, one an artifact of a time when life was endlessly romantic (see: constant copulation), the other a hope of things to come (see: constant copulation while staring into each other’s eyes). They deserved to share the same space, the same air...the same sunlight.

Agnes rose from her desk, her face aglow, her tight sweater resplendent, her trim, young form dreaming of a romantic evening spent with Leonard and his apologizing for ever deciding to leave her for no one in particular.

She discovered, however, that there was no room on the tiny window sill for the flowers. The small pot which the cactus called home was already protruding almost half an inch off of the tiny perch, and the roses were too long at any rate. Not that they were long stem roses, as there was nothing long about those flowers in the least.

She thought for a moment, then plucked the cactus from its unsteady shelf and turned to her desk.

* * *

To Jean, it was not so much of a turn as it was a spin. The younger girl radiated beauty and health and life and everything else which, at that juncture in Jean's life, represented evil.

This was the type of vile woman that had trapped Leon Burkett in a loveless marriage devoid of affection or "Love Amongst the Daisies" or any sort of happiness at all. Her, spinning around, sunlight reflecting off her rosy cheeks (not sunlight, so much as it was the fluorescent lighting), her golden hair whipping about and settling upon her shoulders, just above her heaving bosom (she was wearing a pushup bra which was half empty in each cup, making them point slightly upward).

This visage of vitality and a future spent with every man on the planet fantasizing about *her* struck Jean with the greatest feeling of disgust and contempt that she had ever felt in her life. Well, okay, except for that one time when she accidentally read one of those sex books with the rather misleading title of "Pirate's Booty". But that feeling had only lasted for the first forty-eight pages, when she initially discovered how much more readable it was when she changed the character's names to hers and Leon's. So this current feeling of disgust and contempt was much stronger.

Jean arose from her seat, her hands trembling with rage. How dare the universe allow such an abomination to continue to exist, how dare fate not have swallowed up this horribly attractive woman with a black hole of ugliness and creepy crawly bugs where her heart should be.

If the Universe, or God, or Buddha or Jehovah or Satan or no other deity was going to do anything about this vile contradiction to all that was safe and sane with the world, then dang it all, Jean Cline would. She stepped away from her desk and stalked toward Agnes, who was making her way back to her desk, roses cradled in her right arm, tiny cactus balanced precariously on the palm of her left.

Still lost in her happy glow of her rediscovered love life, Agnes did not notice Jean's approach, nor the fury or hatred which rolled off the other woman like waves on a violent ocean. She did not even register the other woman's presence until Jean grabbed her by the shoulder and spun her around.

Her initial intention was to give the vile woman a piece of her mind, but when she spun Agnes around, the cactus flew from Agnes's hand and hit Jean squarely in the neck. It stuck there, hanging on by it's tiny, mostly ineffective thorns (in defense of the cactus, it was the angle with which it hit that kept it hanging on, and had nothing to do with any ill intent felt by the mostly innate plant).

There was a brief moment of shock as Jean marveled at the thought of this evil woman drawing first blood, then she recovered before the dreamy look on that harlot's face could melt away entirely. By instinct alone, Jean punched Agnes in the gut, which doubled her over, expelling the breath from her lungs in one giant whoosh, but also caused the action of doubling over to drive her forehead into Jean's nose.

Blood exploded from the older woman's broken nose, drenching the front of her Ship and Shore blouse and the back of Agnes's blonde hair.

Chad from Accounting raced over to help—oh, take a wild guess. When it is an older woman and a younger one fighting, who is the man going to try and protect first?

He put a hand on Agnes's shoulder to try and turn her away from Jean, who was doing her best to give the other woman a bloody shower. Agnes felt the touch on her shoulder and fully expected another attack. She whipped the roses out and upward, trying to fend off the imagined attack.

The thorns on the stems caught Chad's left cheek and laid it open. He staggered backward, hand trying to stem the flow of blood which was now leaking from his previously un-maimed face, and bumped into the desk of Joe Gray, another member of Accounting that had been after the

Vice President of Accounting's job for the last two years.

Joe had been overlooked by management for three promotions thus far, all of which had gone to younger candidates. Chad was younger, and now Chad had splashed Joe's coffee (yes, I know exactly how 'Joe's coffee' sounds, but I'm just relating the facts here, okay?) over the reports Joe was almost finished typing up for the President of Accounting. The reports had taken him the better part of two days, and almost two entire bottles of correction fluid, so you can imagine Joe's sudden fury at the ruination of several hours' worth of work.

As if the reports weren't enough, Chad also had the audacity of dripping blood into the opening at the top of Joe's electric typewriter. Joe saw it fall directly onto the black ribbon, and he knew if he tried typing now, the imprint from the keystrokes would be an angry red, not the uniform and pleasant black which was expected on all reports that were requested by the President of Accounting.

He grabbed Chad's tie and gave it a yank, hoping the action would bury the other man's head into the typewriter so Joe could start typing "CHAD IS A DICK" all over the man's bleeding face. Yet Chad, who had yet to figure out how to tie a proper Windsor knot, wore clip-on ties—it tore away from the top of his shirt, which incensed Joe even further. He stood up and gave him a great shove.

Chad careened into Charles Vee—one of the data entry infiltrators—who was Vietnamese and had only been in the country for eight months. To say that Charles wasn't popular would be an understatement to his situation; at a time when the entire country was still trying to heal from the Vietnam conflict, the poor man was an outsider, to some an enemy by association. When you consider what he had to go through in his life before immigrating to America, Charles' life thus far had surmounted that of anyone else in the entire building. Life had been exceedingly difficult in his native country, so much so that his entire family, so far as he knew, was dead at the hands of the North Vietnamese. He had seen far more violence than anyone should ever be witness to, had suffered more loss in his thirty-three years than someone should have to during their entire lifetime.

So when Chad crashed into him from behind, Charles Vee reacted naturally—he spun in his chair, adding momentum to the fist he had instantly raised. It caught Chad squarely in the jaw (as if it hadn't already taken enough punishment, it happened to be on the cheek which had already been pimp-slapped with half-a-dozen Do Me roses) and sent him stumbling back in the direction of Joe.

Charles Vee, horrified at the blood on his fist and the violence he had just committed, jumped up from his desk and ran from the open office floor. In his haste, he bumped into Carlos Viega, who inadvertently fell against Myra Hutchins, a large woman that enjoyed arm wrestling, drinking beer, and manhandling her ninety-pound husband.

She let Carlos know exactly what she felt about him (another of the dirty data entry bastards) and the rest of his kind taking jobs from upstanding Americans (even though he had been born in The Bronx, his mother had been born in Miami and his father in New Mexico). She relayed this message with her fists, and when he tried backing away from her, he bumped into...okay, you get the picture. All hell was breaking loose.

On the other side of the room, Jean Cline and Agnes Fisk looked each other in the eyes. Jean's nose was still bleeding freely, and Agnes was just getting her breath back.

Carefully pulling the cactus from the side of her neck, Jean gave the most menacing, hate-filled look that she could muster. "Ooo boke my nobse," she said.

Agnes was immediately puzzled. "What?"

"Ooo bwoke my nodes," Jean tried growling, but it sounded almost as ridiculous the second time around. She held up the tiny, almost completely innocent cactus. "Amb ooo are gong to eat thish, bish!"

Agnes shook her head slightly. "I have no idea what you're saying."

Jean screamed in fury and cocked her arm back. She intended to shove the cactus down the throat of the evil, vile, black widow killer skank before her, but Agnes realized her intent and slashed out with the roses again. Rose petals exploded across Jean's face; she flinched back involuntarily and dropped the cactus to the desk behind her.

She reached out blindly and grabbed hold of the thorny stems, and ripped the flowers from Agnes's hands. The pain from the thorns digging into her fist barely registered to the woman; she lashed forward, punching her in the eye and sending her reeling.

All about the office, fights were raging. Charles Lee had made it to the stairwell relatively safe, but Carlos was trying to mount an offensive against the angry fists belonging to one decidedly racist Myra Hutchins, who soon found herself trying to fight off Mariela Rodriguez, who could no longer stand by and watch her Hispanic compatriot get beaten down by such an offensive bigot. Mariela, who spoke very little English, didn't need to understand the hateful words and slurs the large white woman was spewing; she only knew that the poor Carlos was practically defenseless because if he hit a white woman, he would most certainly be deported, and Mariela (who was in the country illegally) was thinking (in Spanish) that there was no greater injustice in the world than to sneak into the land of freedom and opportunity only to be summarily beaten for your efforts to earn an honest living.

Chad and Joe were busy slapping each other and anyone in their immediate vicinity. Neither of the men could see all that well anymore—Joe's glasses had been knocked from his face by a flying shoe a few moments earlier, and Chad was trying to get correction fluid out of his eyes—so both were just swinging at any blurry thing that moved. They were successful in knocking out two women who had been racing for the stairwell, and getting three other men involved in the fracas, one of whom had just gotten his brown belt in karate and had been awaiting a moment to use his newfound skills. Unfortunately, when he was setting his legs in the proper stance, he was kicked in the crotch by Betty Tatem from Marketing; Betty was wearing pointy high heels, so when she landed the kick, it took Jack Lapson a full thirty seconds to muster a scream and crumple to the floor.

Betty wound up getting slapped by Joe Gray when he went into windmill mode after Chad landed a solid slap that bloodied Joe's lip. The Windmill Move connected with only three other people (Chad was not one of them) before he managed to break his hand on one of the sturdy desks. He went to his knees, cradling his broken right hand, crying at the pain and the fact that the only way was he getting that freaking report done now was if he hired someone else to do it.

Screams of fury and pain arose across the

third-floor office. Staplers and tape dispensers flew, blood sprayed and dripped, anger raged and harsh language was dispensed as heartily as fists were being thrown. Yet Agnes Fisk and Jean Cline heard none of it—they were too busy strangling each other.

Neither could acknowledge the fact that they were at a deadlock in the choking department. Both squeezed the other's neck as tightly as they could; even as black spots began dancing in their vision, they would not relinquish their holds.

And when they both fell to the ground unconscious, the battles about them raged on.

* * *

Leonard showed up at Price, Montgomery, and Cash around five-thirty—half an hour later than when he was supposed to. He had had to stop at a nearby drug store to buy condoms and breath mints, both of which were entirely necessary to protect the women he came in contact with.

He made it up to the third floor before he was stopped by a police officer, of which there were many present. The office looked as though it had been hit by a tornado—desks were overturned, shattered glass littered the ugly carpet, and paramedics sat with people who looked dazed, as if they had been in a horrible car accident or a plane crash. They were bandaging wounds, telling people to hold ice packs to their heads, and in several cases administering shots.

Leonard took all of this in but did not immediately wonder what had happened. He was much more concerned about finding Agnes and getting the weekend started, quite possibly in the parking garage next door. He had taken the bus, but the garage appeared semi-private, and at this point, Leonard was ready to do it in a cave underwater if necessary. He was a desperate and exceedingly horny man.

"Can't go in there buddy, the whole place is a crime scene."

He glanced down at the hand pressing against his chest, then back up at the officer. "I need Agnes Fisk," he said.

The policeman looked down at a clipboard, then looked back up at him. "She's been taken to the Mercy General E.R. You know where that is?"

Leonard nodded, but his head was reeling. She was in the emergency room of a hospital. He finally began to glance around at the bruised, bloodied, and broken people of Price, Montgomery, and Cash, and realization began to dawn on him.

"Oh my God," he said. "Is it bad?"

The officer shook his head. "No idea, Bub."

"Is it..." Leonard swallowed, not wanting to know but desperately needing to. "Was it her face?"

The cop glared at him.

"I mean," Leonard said, rolling his eyes and blushing, "was it her mouth? We have a big weekend planned."

"Go to the hospital and find out, dickhead. Just get out of here." Shaking his head, the cop turned away from him to consult with a fellow officer.

Leonard just stood there, taking it all in, still not fully comprehending what he was seeing. All he knew was that if Agnes wasn't going to be able to perform this weekend, his efforts would be better spent with one of the ladies down at the wharf.

He was turning to go when a man with broken glasses and coffee stains and blood down the front of his shirt approached him. "You Agnes Fisk's boyfriend, ain'tcha?"

Leonard nodded and was about to ask if her mouth was okay when the man held something out to him. "Make sure she gets this, would ya? She seemed to care about it an awful lot."

Leonard took what was being offered—it was a little cactus in a tiny white pot. He noticed flecks of blood all over the green plant and suddenly realized that if that was Agnes's blood, he probably did not want to see her this weekend. Being the utter and complete douche that he was, Leonard went to hand the plant back to the man that had given it to him, but he was already gone.

He took one last look around, just to see if he could spot a cute girl that needed rescuing. Not seeing any, he left the building, cactus in one hand, and a useless bag of prophylactics in the other. He headed in the direction he was pretty sure the hospital was not in, and after several blocks found himself in front of the place he had stumbled into three months ago, looking for something that would endear Agnes Fisk to him for as long as it took to get her naked.

He entered and approached the desk of the quaint little thrift store, looking down at the cactus as he did so.

He noticed that there was no longer any blood on it at all. Even the white pot was clean, and that freaked Leonard out.

* * *

After leaving the thrift store, Leonard went straight to the hospital to see Agnes. A sudden, inexplicable change had come over him, one which he would later attribute to the bloody aftermath of whatever had occurred in the offices of Price, Montgomery and Cash.

All he knew was that was done with the unknown, and needed something familiar and loving in his life.

Luckily for Agnes Fisk, he met Jean Cline in the lobby as she was leaving, and fell instantly and madly in love with her, which could have been because he could not understand a word she was saying through the splint on her nose. And the neck brace holding her head eerily erect was something he found oddly erotic. But more than likely it was because she was holding a romance novel.

And had folded down the corners of the pages where the sexy parts were.

ANDREA'S PROBABILITY

The alien invasion took place in the business district at lunch hour. You'd think that everyone would have noticed something as monumental as an alien invasion immediately—it wasn't as though Hollywood hadn't been warning everyone for the several decades leading up to that warm summer day—but no one did. At least, not until it was too late. Alas, the vast majority of them were all staring down at their smartphones.

Except for Sean Bigsly—he was reading a book while enjoying his noontime respite, sitting on a bench in the little park out front of the Mason & Tonic Financial Building, trying his damnedest not to drip mango salsa on the pages. He didn't work at that building, he just loved that little bench under the elm there, and rushed there every day at 11:55 so he could claim it before anyone that actually worked in that building did.

On that particular day, he was successful in

not dripping his lunch from the Taco Bucket upon the treasured words of one Stephen King; rather, it was his brains that destroyed the spotlessness of said book when the first shot of the day was fired. Brain-spatter will most certainly destroy the pristine integrity of any book, and that particular tome, and perhaps in glory of the gore contained within the words, was no exception.

The only person that did notice the perfectly circular UFO circling over the city was Andrea Thompson, recently unemployed by Jakes & Stanton Securities on the fifth floor of the Mason & Tonic Financial Building. She was walking outside with the contents of her cubicle tucked inside a copy-paper box. If she hadn't been so humiliated five minutes prior, she probably would have missed the invasion herself. As it was, she noticed through her teary eyes the shadow of the colossal ship fall across the framed photo which was at the top of her rather light and mostly empty box of personal effects. The picture was from the trip she had taken to Hawaii six years ago for vacation. By herself.

The photo was nestled inside a small, wooden, unfinished frame she had found at a little boutique in midtown a few years ago. At the time, she was desperately depressed by all of the personal negativity she harbored about her weight, her height, her plainness. Everything that looked back at her in the mirror every morning and every night had been weighing on her (no pun intended).

The picture had been pinned to the refrigerator by one of those magnets the real estate agents send you in the mail. Her mother had mailed the magnet to her from Florida, along with stationery from a Holiday Inn, two broken seashells, and a ten dollar gift card to McDonald's, all for one of her birthdays. Big spender, mom was.

It was during that time of depression that she stared at the picture with hatred. Hatred at the plump girl with the fake smile that peered back at her, hatred for the time during her life she felt was being wasted on diet plans backed up by boxes of Twinkies and cartons of Ben & Jerry's. One day, as she set aside a half-eaten Teriyaki Chicken with Fat-Free Sauce and Rice with Bamboo Chutes and Peas, and replaced it with a Whoopi Pie, she sat with the framed photo in her lap, thinking about that trip she had taken to Hawaii. (By herself.) As she thought about chances not taken and opportunities that had never presented themselves, a small piece of chocolate from the Whoopi Pie fell on the glass. Using her thumb to wipe the chocolate off, she wound up smearing it across the photo. Now it looked like a picture of a chubby girl with poo on her face.

From that moment forward, she used that photograph as motivation for change. She did not want to be that mousy fat girl anymore. She did not want to live out the rest of her life scared of everything and too shy to speak her mind or take chances. She no longer wanted to live vicariously through romance novels and binge-watching Lifetime movies.

The picture was of her on the zip line on one of the smaller islands. She was smiling, but it was not a happy smile. It was a "get me the hell out of this freaking harness" smile. She had chickened out of the zip line as soon as the picture was taken. The chasm was too deep, the forest too thick, the wildlife calling out all about her too loud, too primal, too unknown.

Truth be told, she had spent the rest of the four days in magical Hawaii in her hotel, getting drunk on Pina Coladas at the pool and hoping that some dark and mysterious native would carry her back to his hut and make love to her for a year. If we are sticking with the absolute truth, it should be mentioned that the closest she got to that particular adventure was a failed attempt at masturbation while watching "How Stella Got Her Groove Back" on the cable TV in her room. Several times. And the "natives", she learned on her second-to-last day on the main island, all spoke English, were actually American citizens, and many took offense when she was able to work up the nerve to utilize the double entendre of winking at them when asking for a "ley".

Again, if we are telling the truth, she only actually dared to use that line one time. Her waiter at IHOP was not impressed, which was why she tipped him fifty-five percent before scurrying back to her hotel room. Where she unsuccessfully tried again at the whole masturbation thing—and she was unsuccessful mainly because the image of her offended waiter "Paul", who really should have had a more tropical name, kept creeping into her head.

Anyways, the alien invasion: she used her shoulders to wipe at her eyes (smearing mascara on her dress, wouldn't you know), then looked straight up into the sky. The ship had a slow rotation to it that did not stop as it came to rest, the center of which looked to be parked somewhere above 42nd St. and Blight Avenue. The end of the giant disc was just above her building, and as she watched, she could see little doors opening up all around the outside bottom edge.

And then laser beams started shooting out of it, and heads began exploding. Andrea figured that that was the best cue she was going to get that she might want to run. She was always good with numbers, and statistics and probabilities began streaming through her head at a breakneck speed. She saw that the killer laser beams were steadily moving closer to her current position, fifty yards away from the doors to the building she had just been escorted from. She saw people starting to look up from their smartphones, only to have their heads blown apart before they could fully grasp what was going on.

She saw lasers firing from the inner sections of the ship at unseen targets deeper in the city.

Obviously not the work of a singular, angry alien. This was a concerted, precise effort. None of the shots were missing. As panic began to spread, and people began to run, the lasers never missed. They hit their targets with an accuracy that meant only one thing: find shelter or die.

She saw all this in a few brief seconds, long enough to know that there was only one place she could go. Andrea spun on her heels and ran for the doors of the building. Others were thinking the same but were not as close as she. Behind her, she could hear the splatters of their heads followed by the crumpling of their bodies.

She was twenty feet from the door when one such splat was closely followed by something warm and sticky plastering the back of one of her calves. With two steps she was out of her heels and leaping up the steps to the main entrance. There were two big, glass doors there, one of which was being opened by one of the security guards that had shown her the way out a minute earlier. He was smiling at her, and shaking his head no. Then he saw what was going on behind her in the plaza, and his expression became one of confusion, and what Andrea immediately assumed was stupidity.

If he hadn't stepped to the side, she would have barreled him over with her copy paper box

The other Rent-a-Cop was turning to see what his partner was doing as Andrea made it past them both, into the large lobby with its fountain and its metal detectors and its leather chairs and sofas and that giant electric stocks ticker that loomed over it all. He turned at just the right moment to see his fake-cop buddy's brains explode from his head, splattering in a wide arc of red and gray and a ludicrous amount of grossness. Then he was stumbling away from the door.

By that point, Andrea was halfway across the lobby. The whole bottom floor was lined with floor-to-ceiling windows, and she wouldn't feel safe unless she was in a bathroom stall. Or the elevator. Or the parking garage beneath the tall building.

She glanced behind her just in time to see the door swing shut (the dead Rent-a-Cop having taken exactly one step outside and then falling to the ground), and a miraculous thing happened: the head-splitting laser beam meant for the second security guard bounced off the glass and ricocheted into the base of the elm in the grassy part of the plaza. The elm seemed to shudder, hesitate, and then collapsed atop the little bench beside it, crushing the body of one recently deceased Sean Bigsly under its considerable weight.

Andrea halted her mad dash across the lobby. When I say "halted", I mean that she stopped running, but her stocking feet carried her another ten yards before her momentum slowed enough for gravity to take over. She came to rest right in the center of one of the walk-through metal detectors, which began to beep incessantly.

"Whoa," she said.

"Holy shit," said security guard number two, who was no longer retreating from the door. "What the hell is going on out there?"

Andrea saw Mike the Janitor entering the lobby area from the direction of the elevators. He was a young man, muscular, with two-day-old scruff on his cheeks, and a patch of manly hair which poked out from the top of his uniform collared shirt. The shirt was two sizes too small, meaning Andrea, if allowed, could stare at that hunk's torso for hours. She had often wondered why he didn't model for the covers of the romance novels she read.

With someone else's head, of course. She thought his body was a perfect specimen, but the slicked-back hair and the giant, hook-like nose kind of ruined the perfect 10 status. And he had a lazy eye. Nothing angered Andrea more than a lazy eye—she was never sure which one she should be looking at when she spoke to people suffering from that affliction, and could never tell if the person was looking back at her or at something off to the left that she couldn't see. Drove her nuts, that did.

"I think—" SG2 started to say, but just then the UFO flashed a barrage of killer laser beams at the door. Thousands of angry red flashes hit the glass, and thousands of the death-dealing cosmic bullets bounced harmlessly off the glass and tore up the dirt and grass of the plaza beyond.

"It's an alien invasion," Andrea said. Her voice sounded huge despite the sound of the alarm from the metal detector, and she shrunk into herself a little at the volume of it. As she tended to avoid any sort of speaking, public or otherwise, the fact that she had spoken like that surprised her.

SG2 looked around at her as if seeing her for the first time. He glanced down at the box, then back up at her face. "Didn't we just kick you out of here?" he asked.

At that precise moment, with his question echoing off the walls, with Mike the Janitor turning to look at her, Andrea changed. She didn't snap, she didn't cry, she didn't go into what her mom called a "conniption fit" and start pounding her feet on the floor.

Her brain decided that with everything she had faced that day, with every obstacle life had thrown at her, with every single thing she had ever failed at—it had all brought her here. To that precise moment, in that exact location. Andrea Thompson was officially done. Done with the daily humiliations and the constant feeling of being weak, of being not quite good enough at anything.

She'd had it.

The part of her that marveled at the strength of other women in books, television, and movies, woke up and said "aw hell no."

The section of her brain that made her

put that photograph in the old frame, the picture of a chubby girl suffering another lost chance, bunched up its muscles and started to flex.

That little resolve that had made her try forty-seven mother humping times to masturbate in her lonely little hotel room in Hawaii for over seventy-two hours stood up and shook its finger at the world.

For the first time in her life, Andrea spoke like she meant to be heard: "Try to kick me out again, and I'll punch your ding-dong."

Both men stared at her for a moment, but before anyone could respond, she turned and completed her journey through the metal detector, which gave two final beeps and fell silent. She strode purposefully to the elevators, head held high, her will resolute and her determination setting her jaw rigid and tight.

She pushed the up button and waited, never glancing back at the two men. This was entirely unnecessary; after an unspoken conversation between the two, they both joined her. That unspoken conversation consisted of them meeting eyes a few times as they looked between each other and the tough-ass broad with the box, although SG2 was unsure if they were speaking about the same thing because one of Mike the Janitor's eyes kept veering off towards the fountain on the far side of the lobby.

"What's the plan, pretty lady?" Mike asked.

"Are we hiding in the basement?" asked

SG2.

Andrea turned and glared at the guard. “Go hide if you want. I’m tired of hiding.”

“So what are we gonna do?” Mike was doing his hey-I’m-looking-at-you-no-I’m-not thing, and that was the final straw.

She shoved the box into his arms and took her picture out. “You are going to hold my box. I’m going to show those aliens who they’re dealing with.”

“Yeah,” said SG2 as the door to elevator number three opened, “I’ll be in the garage.”

Andrea entered the elevator, thought for a moment, then grabbed Mike and pulled him in after her. “I need you to swipe your security card so I can get to the roof access.”

He gaped at her. “You’re serious?”

“As serious as...” Her brain took a second to process. “As serious as herpes,” she said, and almost smiled at herself. Two sex-related references in under five minutes, and out loud, to boot.

As the door to the elevator slid closed, he took his security badge from his pocket and pushed it into the slot at the bottom of the panel with all the buttons on it. When a little green light came on, he pushed the button marked “25” and stepped back.

“This won’t go all the way to the roof. But from the twenty-fifth floor, we can take the access stairs up to the top.”

The elevator started to rise, and she could

see him looking her up and down, his gaze admiring, as if seeing her for the first time. Which he probably was; there were so many beautiful women that worked in this building, who would ever notice mousy old Andrea Thompson?

She was just starting to wonder if he would scream "RAPE!" if she grabbed him by the shirt and planted a big juicy one on his lips when the elevator dinged and stopped on the fifth floor. The door slid open, and standing there was Marcia Bogden, her ex-employer. She took a step forward and stopped dead in her tracks when she saw Andrea.

Marcia Bogden was one of those fortyish women who spent her money on Botox and liposuction and dressed in the shortest of skirts. Her tops were always open to the lowest possible button the human resources department would allow; since HR was run by two old men, her neckline started somewhere above her navel but most definitely stopped someplace under her fake breasts.

During the entire four minutes that Marcia had taken out of her busy day of flirting with upper management and condescending to all lower employees to fire Andrea, she had been smiling. An honest to goodness, happy frigging smile. Like she enjoyed nothing more than to prey on the innocent and the weak.

What Marcia didn't realize was that she was now standing before the new Andrea.

"I was damn good at my job, you know," Andrea announced.

Marcia smirked and said, "And yet there you are, holding a box of your personal effects. Why are you back? Did you forget something, dear?"

"Yes," Andrea replied. "Your two-thirty canceled. Said he had a doctor's appointment because you gave his ding-dong herpes."

The universe was smiling on Andrea that day; no sooner were the words out of her mouth than the doors were sliding shut on a speechless Marcia. As the elevator began its ascent again, she glanced at Mike the Janitor.

A smile was slowly forming on his face. "That woman is a major bitch," he said. "That was awesome."

She grinned sheepishly, then remembered that this was a new her, who didn't gloat when she got in a zinger. She could giggle about it later. Maybe.

"You know nobody says that anymore, though."

Her brow furrowed. "What?"

"Ding-dong. Nobody says 'ding-dong'."

"Oh," she said, her resolve faltering briefly. "What do they say?"

His face flushed, and he looked down at the ground—which was a relief, as he was doing that thing with the eye again, and Andrea had seriously been considering slapping his head to see if she could get it to go straight. "They're bad words, ma'am."

She wondered what the feeling was that was sweeping over her. If she had ever felt it before, she would have realized she was physically responding to what her brain perceived as flattery. Mike the Janitor had just complimented her by not wanting to say bad words to her. In her mind, she suddenly saw him on the front of one of those romance novels. Only he was in profile, so you couldn't see that one bad eyeball. And his nose had been photoshopped.

"It's okay, Mike, I'm a big girl now."

His face turned even redder. He mumbled something, and she had to ask him to repeat it. "Dick!" he said, a little too loudly. She did giggle then. And glanced at the electric counter on the elevator, which said "18".

And then she reached over, grabbed a handful of Mike's uniformed shirt, and yanked him over to her. The box of all of her work things kept them from colliding, and also kept his face too far from hers.

"Drop it," she said, and he did, and the box landed on her feet, but she didn't care. She yanked him the rest of the way to her, planting her mouth over his and sticking her tongue so far into his mouth she felt like she was pulling a muscle.

But oh, it was a good burn. It didn't matter that she had to turn her head sideways to avoid his monstrous nose. It didn't matter that something was leaking on her foot through the bottom of the box. It didn't matter that his one eye was not staring back at hers...

...okay, that mattered. She broke the kiss long enough to gasp for breath and say "Close one of your eyes!", and then she was diving back in.

She had never once wondered whether she was a good kisser or not, as her experience in that department had consisted of Joey Pong, a Vietnamese exchange student, in the seventh grade (no tongue, just braces that had banged painfully together), and Mark Jessup at the Homecoming dance her senior year (which had involved so much tongue and spit that she asked him afterward if he had an extra saliva gland or two, and he'd never spoken to her again—she hadn't even meant it insultingly, she had genuinely been curious). So when the elevator dinged and the door opened onto the twenty-fifth floor, she pushed him away and did not wait for a response.

She straightened the big bow on her blouse, winked at him, and strode from the elevator, a steely, determined look in her eye.

Watching her go, Mike the Janitor wiped her drool off of his chin and decided that now was definitely not the time to tell her he was gay.

* * *

They stood at the top of the stairs. Andrea had her

hand on the door handle, and Mike had his card ready to plunge into the slot.

New Andrea saw that double meaning, wrapped it up in a pretty little bow, and stored it into the part of her brain that she imagined looked just like her vagina. She had definite plans for him when she got back.

"You sure you want to do this?" he asked her. "You don't even know if whatever it is you plan on doing is gonna work."

She gave him a cocky smile. "Never know unless you try. Now plunge that card in my slot, mister. I mean, stick it in the hole. Wait...just swipe the damn card," she finally managed, her resolve not faltering in the least.

He did, and when the light turned green, she gave him one last, deep look (into his right eye, because the other one seemed to be reading the "In Case of Emergency" sign next to the fire extinguisher) and said: "I've got little alien dicks to kick."

She shoved the door open and jumped out onto the roof, holding the frame directly over her head. Mike the Janitor, no dummy, yanked the door shut behind her.

Above her, she saw one of the little doors open. Being this much closer to the alien spacecraft, she could see all of the lines and pipes and hatches that lined the bottom of the ship. None of it, not the technology, not the symmetrical construction, not the plain old giant size of it, mattered to her.

Just that open door, and the little red light inside of it, the light that was slowly growing brighter. She braced herself, expecting an impact.

When the Laser Beam of Death struck the glass that protected the photograph of her failed attempt at bravery in Hawaii, there was no jolt, no force behind it. It bounced off the 4x5 pane, and if she hadn't been looking, she would not have even known it had hit her intended target.

Andrea was all about mathematics. She was all about angles and statistics and physics. So the adjustment she made to the angle of the frame was just slight enough so that no one else would notice. She was an expert when it came to numbers, and she knew just the right angle to make so that when the laser beam which was meant to splatter her noggin hit the glass, it would go right back to where it came from.

As the shot entered the hatch and therefore the inside of the ship, Andrea screamed as loud as she could, hoping against hope that some little green bastard—whom she imagined was probably addicted to liposuction and Botox—would hear.

"EAT MY ASS-HAT, YOU INVADER PRICK HOLES!"

Again, universe smiling and all, a jet of flame so large it singed her eyebrows off erupted from the open porthole. The ship seemed to give a giant shudder and then began to move slowly away from her, as though it were trying to run away.

Then came a deafening roar as every hatch and door and window on the ship exploded, sending metal and panels and what looked like packaging peanuts flying. She felt someone grab the back of her shirt and pull hard, and suddenly she was back on the landing at the top of the stairs and Mike the Janitor was slamming the metal door shut.

They could hear all sorts of shrapnel pinging against the door and the roof of the building. When a long, sharp piece pierced the door and wedged itself into the floor between Mike's legs, they decided to go down a few floors. Fast.

* * *

They stared at each other—well, okay, Mike was staring at two different things at once, but one of them was our heroine, which is the important thing.

They looked at each other uncomfortably.

"I'm sorry," she said. "I didn't know."

He waved her apology away. "How could you? It's not like I wear a name tag that says 'Mike the Gay Janitor' or something."

"Well, I'm sorry I mouth raped your face."

He smiled at her. "If it's any consolation, I was kinda flattered. Haven't been kissed like that in a long time. Well...never, really, not like *that.*"

"Was it bad?" she asked, more embarrassed now than she had been when he had carefully but forcefully removed her hand from his crotch thirty seconds ago.

"Well, you're a girl. So I can't actually compare..." He fell silent for a moment as he struggled with something.

"Oh, just say it," she said. "I can take it. The old me would probably have cried for a week, but not me now—I just killed a freaking spaceship."

"Okay," he said. "I just don't want you to be offended or anything."

"I'm good," she said.

"Do you have, like, an extra saliva gland or something?"

"You think the security guard is still in the garage?" Andrea asked after a slight hesitation.

"Probably. You want a condom?"

"I'd love one," she answered.

Mike the Gay Janitor put his card in the slot, then pushed the "B" button.

* * *

Andrea kept the frame on her nightstand. It was the same picture as before. Still the one of the zip line, starting above her head and disappearing into the forest in the background. Still, the fake smile. Still, her looking off to the left.

Only now there was a scorch mark in the glass next to her face. Now, it looked like she was looking to the side, at the giant burn in the glass. It seemed as though she was looking right at it, with that wary smile, and it seemed that no longer she was thinking "what the hell am I doing?".

Now it looked like she was thinking "screw you, alien laser beam."

BULLETS AND TIME

Ever have one of those moments when you wish that you had brought that one last grenade?

It doesn't even have to be a grenade—maybe it was a credit card, or a certain set of keys. It could have been something as simple as a quarter, just some spare pocket change. What matters is that you looked at it as it sat on your dresser or your kitchen table or in the case of ammunition you keep under your bed, your hand hesitating over it, wondering, *will I need that?*

Should I take it? You know, just in case?

Yes.

You should.

* * *

"He's out of ammo."

Pritchard glanced at Franks, smirking. "Then why don't you go get him?"

His partner swallowed. Sweat was running freely down the side of his face, sweeping droplets of blood along with it. Some of it was his, most of it was not. They were huddled behind three large crates marked "machine parts"; the warehouse was full of them, most of them now punctured with bullet holes. On the far side of the room, one of the crates had been blown apart and was still smoking. Whether he was out of ammunition or not, Pritchard was not taking any unnecessary chances if the man was packing grenades. That was a whole other level of business, if you asked him.

"He's been quiet for ten minutes now. He's either dead, or he's out of ammo."

Pritchard chuckled. "Guys like him don't die easy. He'd go loud, and with a big bang."

"Then he's out of ammo," Franks hissed, irritated and angry and impatient. "We could take him now."

The older of the two gestured with his pistol—which had a full clip in it, thank you very much—and repeated: "Then why don't you go get him?"

Franks mumbled something, then checked his own clip for the hundredth time.

Pritchard hated being paired with a kid on a job like this, but it wasn't like he had a choice. If the boss gave you an assignment, you did exactly what you were told. All things being said, he would rather be at home with the wife and kids, baking Christmas cookies and watching "Rudolph" or trying to concoct a combination of eggnog and liquor that he could actually stomach.

"What'd you say?"

Franks spun around and glared at him. "I said I'm tired of this, why isn't he doing anything, and what the hell are we waiting for?"

Pritchard shook his head. "Maybe he wants you to think he's out of ammo. Maybe he's just low and wants to pick us off one by one. By the way, raising your voice will give away your position. Might want to keep it down, Junior."

His partner clenched his jaw, his fist noticeably tightening around the grip of his nine millimeter. "You think you know so much," he muttered.

"I'm forty-three years old, kid."

"So? What's your age have to—"

"I've been doing this job for twenty-five years, and I'm still alive, aren't I?"

Franks' mouth snapped shut. He looked away, towards the office door, then down at the floor. "Just tired is all."

Pritchard nodded and, reaching out, squeezed the kid's shoulder. "We all are, kid."

He returned his gaze to the darkened office. Bullets had blown out the big bay window, and the metal door itself was riddled with holes. The only thing that had saved the man trapped inside was the concrete walls surrounding him. But they had him cornered—only one door, only one window, both on the same wall.

He glanced at his watch; it had been twelve minutes since the last shot had been fired. The next person who pulled a trigger would more than likely die from the effort. Pritchard could think of no better way to give your position away than with a loud noise.

"Still think he's out of ammo," the kid said.

* * *

Yeah, one grenade would do it. Nothing causes panic like a bouncing metal pineapple of death.

That one I had chosen not to take this morning. For the life of me, I cannot even recall why I didn't grab it. Could have been because I was worried about the extra weight, could be because I thought three would be enough, could be because I was just too lazy to affix another one to my belt. The reason doesn't really matter.

What matters is that it was not some quarter or keys. It was an explosive. There's nothing saying I would not have already used it, but seriously, why ponder the philosophical what-ifs of the entire thing? I chose not to take it. My decision.

The only bad one of the day, yet still mine.

Every other action, every step taken, every bullet fired—each done because I planned for it to happen. I planned the trajectory and destination of every shot and every footfall. No wasted motion, no wasted ammunition.

Except, of course, for the *grenade* I chose *not* to take. *That* is what I would call wasted ammunition....

* * *

Pritchard peered around the crate, cursing softly.

"See—Gus thinks he's out of ammo, too," the kid said from over his shoulder.

"Gonna get himself killed, just watch." Pritchard shifted his position, tracking Gus's movement to the office door. The big man was inching up slowly along the wall, trying to be as quiet as possible, his gun held in both hands and pointed at the floor.

"If Gus makes it in, I'm going to help."

"No, kid, you are not." Pritchard shook his head. "Not if you want to live."

"C'mon, man, we should be backing him up right now instead of hiding behind boxes like a bunch of cowards." He moved as if to stand and it was all Pritchard could do to not shoot the kid himself.

"You take one step out there, you're dead.

He has a clear line of sight on you, and he can't see Gus. Now shut up, you're too damn loud."

"But he's out of frigging ammo!" the kid cried, and that's when a shot rang out.

The bullet took off the top of Franks' head. He got a confused look on his face, then fell back to the ground.

Pritchard sat staring at the kid's body for a moment, then made a silent vow to see this thing through and to kill this son-of-a-bitch first chance he got.

* * *

Then again, grenades can be a hindrance. You have to time them just right—the last thing you need is some agile person throwing it back at you so that it explodes in your face and not the other, the more preferable way around.

You have to pull the pin, release the safety lever, count the seconds off depending on the distance to the target, and let it fly. If you do it right, and some gutsy moron catches it...well, nice catch, but you should have let that one go past you, bub. Bye-bye, upper torso.

The mechanics of them are pretty simple, pretty straightforward. It can be easy to figure out how to use something that will blow you to kingdom come—the trick is learning how to use it so that it doesn't. Even with something as basic as a grenade, you need training. Screw it up once, training is over. I have more respect for a grenade than I do for a gun. Granted, both take a fair amount of hand-eye coordination, but with a grenade, you just have to get it to land in the general area for it to be effective. Guns you train for with years to get to the level I'm at—decades, really.

So, yeah. Today, I'm missing that extra grenade. Could have shortened this job up nicely. Pritchard felt the disconnect coming on.

He didn't swallow his emotions so much as he forcibly choked them back down, like bile. It left an acidic taste in his mouth, burning his throat, snapping his analytical mind into wakefulness. He turned from Franks' corpse, staring down the darkened hole of the office window.

Watched as Gus reached for the doorknob, then gripped it tightly, turning it slowly, gun pointed at where the door would open. Pritchard knew that Gus had given his position away before his hand had even brushed the knob—his big body, passing in front of the door that had earlier been struck by several bullets, would have blocked any light shining through the holes.

Pritchard stared into the dark room, waiting for the muzzle flash.

Gus opened the door no more than an inch, and the man within the office fired. Without hesitation, Pritchard fired twice, once to the right of the flash, and again at the left. At the same time, Gus pulled the door shut as hard as he could, then retreated to his own stack of boxes, his hand patting his body for wounds, which Pritchard was glad to see were absent. He'd gotten off lucky; the man holed up in that office was one hell of a shot, and had steadily diminished their team to himself, Gus, and Palto, who was waiting outside to make sure there was no escape.

The sound of the last shots faded slowly into the recesses of the warehouse. An eerie silence fell over them, one that Pritchard was hesitant to break.

Then he heard coughing from within the office. The only sound the man inside it had made since he had slammed the door shut behind him ages ago.

"Nice shot," came the voice from the darkened office.

Pritchard didn't answer; if it was a ploy to give up his position, he was far too seasoned to fall for it. Not today, buddy.

"Punctured a lung with that one," the man called out. There was silence for a moment, then the sound of metal hitting the floor. "Shit." Then came a cry of pain. "Dropped my lighter."

Pritchard's eyes narrowed, but he was not about to peek over the box---especially not after what had happened to Franks. But what was this guy doing?

There was a slight scraping sound from the

office, then a grunt. "Do me a favor, pal. Don't shoot. I'm going to light up a cigarette."

Pritchard heard the familiar sound of a Zippo, then caught the reflection of a flame in the small, cloudy window that ran above where the big bay window had been. He glanced over at Gus, who had a better view of the room. The big man shrugged, then pantomimed smoking.

"Huh," he said involuntarily. One last sm—

* * *

Now that I think about it, perhaps it was by design that I didn't pick up that extra grenade.

Like someone—or some*thing*—from on high was looking down on me. Totally made me not even consider taking it. Maybe my eyes just moved past it and I grabbed something else instead.

Maybe I wasn't meant to bring it. Maybe it would have changed the outcome of this already screwed up day. For the better, or the worse—did that even matter? If today was my day to die, who the hell was I to question that one last grenade?

Funny to think about it, but I'm just a little person in the grand scheme of things. Aren't we all?

* * *

The shot took Pritchard in the neck.

A small piece of the box he was hiding behind had been blown off earlier, and it was the only view of him the man in the office had. It was an expert shot, not one that too many people in this city could make, especially with a handgun.

A great arc of blood shot out from behind the box, painting the floor beyond with a thin, angry splash. Pritchard struggled to a standing position, turning and pointing his gun at the dark office, his free hand going to the wound in an attempt to staunch the flow. But the blood continued to leak from him, a steady flow of life which was leaving his vision dark.

He opened his mouth to say something—his intention was a threat, or maybe a curse word. Something to express his rage at his sudden fate.

All that came out was the word "cookies," then he was slipping in his blood, falling over the box, and dying. The gun slipped from his hand left hand, and the right fell away from his neck. He thought again about the kids and "Rudolph," and then he simply ceased to think.

The office door opened slightly, then wider. The man stepped up to the doorframe, leaning against it as he considered Pritchard's body.

"Sorry, buddy," he whispered, then

coughed, spraying blood across the floor. "Couldn't let my last bullet go to waste." He took two steps out of the office and heard the hammer of a gun clicking to his right.

Gus leveled the nine-millimeter at him and said, "Good thing I got one left," and pulled the trigger.

* * *

Two hours later, Gus noticed the bullet lodged in the journal he had picked up at the train station gift shop yesterday. He had put the leather-bound, blank book in his inside jacket pocket, and had forgotten he had placed it there.

Until he had been gathering ammunition that morning, and even then it wasn't the journal itself he had taken note of, so much as that he didn't have a free spot for that fourth grenade.

INTERLUDE: BOB THE DOG

None of the other dogs ever wanted to hang around Bob, but this really never affected him. Every day when he was let outside, he was free to roam the city, and that was all that he was ever concerned about. Running through the clean streets of the city center, chasing birds; dashing through the business district, racing after the few squirrels who lived there, never catching one but always thrilling in the chase.

Down by the wharf he would sniff at the air, trotting with a wary eye past the men who lived in the dark corners there. He would strut past the whores who plied their trade in the better-lit areas of that region, wagging his tail at them and barking confidently, as if to say he could have any of them if he wanted, but he was a very busy dog, and must be on his way.

If he encountered any other dogs, this was usually the place for such meetings. Bob always saw them before they caught sight of him, but upon approach, they already knew he was coming. His scent, carried to them upon the air, was what put them off. He never got close enough for a greeting; they'd catch his scent, turn and see him, and scamper off with nary a growl or bark.

Again: Bob was nonplussed by these encounters. He could not help the way he'd been made, could he?

He would walk south, to the college, and roll around in the lush grass of the plazas there, and occasionally pause to stare into the fountain with the big statue. There were shiny things at the bottom of the water there that always mesmerized him, until some student would remark upon him or try to pet him. He would always run from them, yet not out of fright. He would run, then spin around, tail wagging. Bob would lower his front end to the ground and bark playfully, as if encouraging them to give chase.

He would roam past the large homes along the river, and stare out across the long bridge which spanned it. He would never go across, though. Bob liked his home, and always returned to it. He would instead follow the river to the edge of where the suburbs began. He would never go down the streets that wound through the neighborhoods there, choosing instead to run along the field which bordered it, chasing after the butterflies that flitted from wildflower to wildflower.

He would be getting tired by the time he came to the main road, and would walk back into the city, sticking to the sidewalks as the street became busier. Past the shops and the restaurants he went, looking at everyone and everything, occasionally stopping to smell the aromas. From the cooking food, the exhaust from the cars, the perfumes of the people—he took in as much as he possibly could.

When the sun began to sink low, he always found himself right back where his journey had begun. The man was always there to pick him up and pat his head, despite his coarse, thickening fur.

Did you see everything I cannot see, Bob? *the man would ask as he cradled him.* Did you smell everything and hear everything which I cannot leave to experience myself?

The man would then carry Bob to his place in the front window, and take the key out of Bob's side and slip it into the compartment on Bob's belly. His memories of the day were already ebbing, receding from him until he was left with only the memory of running. That memory was enough; it made him pose rigidly in front of the window until the sun rose on a new day.

Good night, Bob, *the man would say, and Bob would sit staring out the plate glass until the man took him out and wound him back up again.*

BLOOD WORK FOR MORTON

Morton stood at the doctor's office window, staring down at the SIGN IN list on the clipboard, and the blue pen that lay next to it. A white string had been tied to the metal clamp of the clip-board, and the other end was taped to the top of the pen. This sight offended him for some reason. He could not bring himself to pick up the pen and write his name down; he had reached for the pen right when he had walked in, but the shade of blue stopped his hand short.

Morton had lowered his hand slowly, already knowing there was absolutely no way in hell he was touching that damned thing. It almost hurt his eyes, that pen, almost hurt him in his *brain*. He could feel it burrowing in there like a fluorescent light that kept getting brighter and brighter. Looking away was not an option--the minute he took his eyes off of it, it would move. Or change. Or disappear. That would be the worst, if it actually went away. Then he would not know where it was, and not being able to see it would surely drive him mad. It could be hiding anywhere.

The fact that the pen was attached to the clipboard, and would have to take that with it, making it that much harder to conceal itself, never occurred to Morton. Nor did it occur to him how ridiculous it was that he found a *pen*—and an innocent blue one, at that —to be nefarious. It was assuredly the most ludicrous idea he'd had all week.

The nurse behind the desk, had she known of his dilemma, would probably have dismissed him as another of the loony hypochondriacs that came through the door every day. Nothing new here, just another paranoid health-care addict.

"Mr. Mosley? Do you need help sir?"

Morton glanced up from the pen, but it was only to make eye contact with her and then he was back at staring down the embodiment of evil. "I..." was all he could produce. He swallowed, but his mouth was dry. An embarrassing clicking sound emanated from his throat. This seemed to break the spell the blue pen had on him; he grinned at her sheepishly and shrugged.

The pretty young nurse smiled and reached for the clipboard. "Don't worry about it, I know you're here. I'll get your chart ready."

Morton leaned over the window, watching her take up the blue pen in her hand. His eyes grew wide, but nothing seemed to happen to her. She scribbled his name on the SIGN IN sheet, looked at her watch, and wrote the time down next to it. The pen did not cut her or cause her to burst into flames, but he still had a sneaky suspicion about it. Something was just not right.

"Has any of your insurance information changed?" she asked. He shook his head no.

"And you're here for some blood work today, correct?"

He started to shake his head "no", but then nodded. "Blood," he said, or tried to; his dry throat was making communication impossible, and the sound that emanated from within him sounded curiously like that of a bullfrog.

"Okay, then have a seat and the nurse will be right with you." She looked up at him and gave him a tight-lipped smile—clearly a dismissal.

His eyes were still fixed on the pen. She glanced down at it, then back at him. "I'll just keep this back here with me," she said, wondering if Mr. Mosley was thinking of filching the pen. He was younger than most of their usual patients, and could be a flight risk. The entire reason for the string and the tape was to discourage the lighter fingered of the elderly, but this one seemed preoccupied with this particular pen. Almost...

...obsessed.

That was when Morton's stomach growled. It was loud enough for her to hear it, and was clearly the root of his issues. Poor man was probably just hungry. She knew she had a hard time functioning in the morning without that first cup of coffee, and he had probably been fasting since last night. Some people just couldn't handle not eating or drinking for a few hours.

"You can go sit, sir," she told him. He smiled, nodded, and sighed, then turned and went to find a seat. She watched him go, shaking her head. Whether he was hungry or a closet kleptomaniac did not matter to her one bit. She went to get his chart and put Morton Mosley out of her mind—with the way things had been in the world lately, they would be busy today with people wanting to get tested for the virus that seemed to be affecting the entire world. Although she had her suspicions that it was just another round of the flu, albeit a rather virulent one.

* * *

Morton stared down at the chair. The cushions were tan and fuzzy. This did not offend him, not like the pen had. Rather, it filled him with a sense of dread. Not that he thought the chair to be evil—it just made him feel that if he sat in it, he would not be getting out of it again.

The waiting room was empty save for one old woman, who was snoring softly in the corner. No one else seemed to notice the indecision and the confusion which held the forty year old man in place. The chair before him beckoned, its welcoming arms trying to entice him to sit. Forever.

"Mr. Mosley?"

He turned his head slowly. He would have turned it faster, but every muscle in his neck was stiff, like he had whiplash. Or like his muscles were covered in glue.

A nurse was standing in the door to his left, holding it open for him. "Just come this way, sir," she said to him. He looked back at the chair and smiled at it.

Almost had me, he thought. He started to turn away, but then remembered the pen. How long ago since he had last seen it? How long had it had to run away to do whatever evil little pens did?

He tried to shake his head to try and clear his

mind; there seemed to be a fog over everything, and he could not concentrate on what he was supposed to be doing: all he could think of was the pen. But trying to shake his head was something his stiff neck would not allow.

His stomach growled again, louder than before, and this seemed to lift the fog a little. He became aware of the nurse still standing there, still holding the door, still waiting.

He went.

* * *

Morton was looking at the name tag clamped to the nurse's chest. "Marjorie" was engraved in black script there, with the letters "RN" at the end.

He glanced around him, and realized he was now sitting. He was in a different room; this one was blazingly white, and smelled of cleaning chemicals and cotton balls and tape. There was a poster on the wall advertising VIAGRA, and one on the opposite wall advertising BIRTH CONTROL. He looked from one to the other, trying to process the mixed messages, forgetting that he had forgotten how he had gotten to this room in the first place.

"Huh," Marjorie muttered. "Did you drink a lot of caffeine yesterday?"

Morton shook his head as much as he was able to. Right now, he wasn't even sure what caffeine was. He knew what VIAGRA was, and he knew what BIRTH CONTROL was, and he was trying to figure out which would be best. Or if there was a certain order in which to take them.

"And you fasted for 12 hours, right? Nothing to eat or drink since eight last night?"

He shook his head again.

"Well," Marjorie sighed. "Your blood just does not want to come out."

Morton looked down and noticed the needle jutting from his arm. He had never felt it go in, and usually he had to look away. As soon as he felt the little stab of pain, he always became nauseous. But not today.

"I'll have to try a baby needle," Marjorie said. She opened an envelope and produced what was, indeed, a baby needle: it was tiny and had a thin plastic tube that came off the end. It reminded him of the blue pen tied to the clipboard, and he glance up at the closed door, expecting to see the pen there, the wooden clipboard dragging behind it.

The pen was not there, however. He looked around the room, his head turning slowly and only part way, but could not find it. There was a cup with two pencils sticking out of the top, and a red magic marker, but no blue pens.

"Are you feeling okay, sir?"

He looked back at Marjorie. His head was already turned in her direction, which was good; if it hadn't been, there would have been an unbearably embarrassing silence as he worked to swivel his head around. He shrugged his response. He wasn't really sure how he felt. He could not recall getting up that morning, or driving to the doctor's office. Morton was surprised that he had even remembered that he *had* an appointment this morning, despite the fact that he had fasted the night before, and had showered before he went to bed. He had even shaved on the off chance that one of the pretty nurses would take notice of him.

The night before an appointment was a big deal for Morton Mosley, but he could not recall a single moment of it. Right now, he saw only two choices.

VIAGRA or BIRTH CONTROL.

Then he noticed the poster on the back of the door. It was for INCONTINENCE. This confounded him even more.

"I'm going to get the doctor," Marjorie said, standing. "I either don't know what I'm doing today, or you are super dehydrated."

He looked at her, and saw the worry on her face. He looked down at his arm, and saw four distinct holes there. They were small, and obviously where she had tried to draw his blood from. He saw the empty vials sitting next to the useless needles on a sheet of thick, blue paper. It was the same shade of blue as the pen. He glanced back up to Marjorie the R.N., but she was already walking to the door.

He looked back down at the blue paper…

* * *

Morton felt a pressure on his arm. It was there suddenly, and pulled his attention away from the blue.

"Mr. Mosley, I asked how you are feeling?"

Slowly he looked up from his right arm and the black band of the blood pressure cuff; his eyes traveled up the white smock, past the name tag which said "Dr. N.

Tillman, M.D.", past the purple tie, past the brown skin of the doctor's neck, and up to his jaw line. He found the doctor's eyes, and found himself shrugging again.

"You seem a bit lethargic today. When is the last time you had anything to drink? Was that yesterday?"

He nodded, his head slowly dropping so he could look at the blue paper again, but stopped at the top of Dr. Tillman's smock, where it brushed against his neck. A vein bulged there--it just happened to be blue. Not like the blue of the pen or the paper, but a deeper, more meaningful blue.

"This is so...*odd*," the doctor said. "I cannot find blood pressure or pulse. It is like...like you are not even..."

He stopped short of completing his sentence and swallowed. He needed to call an ambulance for this man. How Mosley was even standing, how he was even communicating...

"Hungry," Morton muttered in a grating voice which did not sound like his in the slightest, and looked back up in the doctor's eyes.

"Well, seeing as how we are not getting any blood from you today, I don't think a little something would hurt you any." Dr. Tillman went to the door and opened it an inch. "Marjorie, could you bring me your breakfast please?"

He glanced back at Morton. "I think she has an apple or something, it's no bother." When the nurse got to the door, Tillman told her softly to call an ambulance. "I don't know what is wrong with him, but he says he is hungry. Wait here a moment."

He walked back to his patient and handed him the apple, which Morton took and stared at. It was red, and hard. Morton was not entirely sure what to do with it.

The doctor walked back to the door, and Marjorie could see the worry and...well, something else she had never seen in the doctor's eyes before. Something that struck a note of fear deep inside there. The other thing she saw in the small doctor's eyes was confusion. He had no idea what was happening to Morton Mosley.

"He is cold to the touch," Tillman said. "And I cannot get a pulse or any of his vitals. It is like...like he is *dead*," Tillman whispered to her. If he saw her shudder at his confirmation of her own fearful thoughts, he did not let on. "Call the ambulance, and wake up Mrs. Gelding in the lobby. Tell her we will have to reschedule."

Marjorie nodded and hurried off, wanting to be away from the room and near to something normal, which was exactly what Mrs. Gelding was: she was old, she was whiny, she smelled of cheese, and she was *normal*.

Dr. Tillman left the door slightly opened as he turned back to his patient, and gasped when he saw that Morton had walked up behind him. "Mr. Mosley, you gave me a start," he said, smiling.

"Blue," Morton tried to say, staring at Tillman's neck.

"What--" was all the doctor could get out; Morton Mosley, who knew his fast was now over, was ravenously hungry. He grabbed the doctor in a tight bear hug and squeezed, pushing the air out of the doctor's lungs. Morton lifted the smaller man, and pulled the pulsing vein to his awaiting mouth. He felt the skin of the doctor's throat on his lips, felt the heat of the other man's life, felt the blood coursing through that vein...

Morton's teeth tore the skin around that pulsing blue vein in Tillman's neck. Blood squirted out in a deep red fountain, and he clamped his teeth around the wound as quickly as he could. New life seemed to flow through him as he worked to keep up with the blood that shot into the back of his throat. The muscles in his neck seemed to relax, and he shook his head against the doctor's neck, tearing out a chunk of his flesh. He moaned his surrender to the hunger that gripped his belly and his brain, and began to chew.

Tillman struggled, but the other man's grip was too strong, and his arms were pinned to his side, and now he could feel his patient biting deeper into his neck, his teeth grinding their way through his muscle. He had no air to scream with. Blood flew from his mouth and splattered on the Viagra poster and the ceiling, and all Tillman could do was watch, watch as his life left him in great, pulsing arcs of red.

His bladder let go, as did all the other muscles in his body. He thought briefly of his wife at home, and the child growing in her belly, and the world fell away from him. The doctor saw the whiteness of the ceiling grow sharper, overpowering the spray of blood.

Then it all went suddenly dark. *We were supposed to watch that new Woody Harrelson movie tonight,* he thought, and died.

* * *

Morton's head flew back, his mouth full of flesh, Dr. Tillman a dead weight in his arms. He chewed, swallowed, and chewed some more. He felt something sticking between his teeth, and worked it out with his tongue. He swallowed the tiny bit of flesh and sighed.

He looked down at the dead doctor, and at the blood drenched floor. For the first time, he noticed a blue pen sticking out of the doctor's bloody shirt pocket. Stomach growling, he considered eating some more. But his jaw was tired from all of the chewing; he had eaten down to the tough shoulder, and had to stop. The muscles and tendons were tough to chew through, and he knew that next time he would have to start with something softer. Like the inside of an arm, or a thigh.

He did not need more to eat at the moment, though; his throat was dry, and what he really needed was to drink. He licked the blood off his fingers absently, and an idea slowly formed in his head.

"Marjorie," he tried calling out. But it came as just a whisper, and did not sound right to his ears. He tried again, his vocal chords straining.

"Breakfast," he tried to say, but all that came out was a click and a moan. He waited for a moment, but no one came. Morton heard a siren in the distance, and when his stomach growled again, he seemed to find his motivation. He staggered to his feet and went to find Marjorie.

The late Dr. N. Tillman opened his eyes and saw the BIOHAZARDS trash can in the corner of the small room.

It was red, but the trash bag lining it was blue. Blue, like a vein.

BIWITCHED

The coven met on Thursday's at nine in a warehouse near the docks, in one of the worst neighborhoods in the city. The ladies—and Randy—looked the part; with the location being in an unsavory place, and being the home of so many unsavory characters, they preferred not to be questioned or confronted.

They wore dark clothing, which typically consisted of black leather, black dresses, black hats, black shoes—except for Randy, who liked to have a little bling on his feet—and a liberal dose of black eyeliner. They tried not to look too fashionable, lest they be targeted by muggers. They tried not to cause too big of a stir, lest they catch the eye of the Holy Catholic Church of Saint Mary of San Cicaro (a raucous crew, those Holy Catholics). They tried not to attract too much attention, lest the local gangs or thugs decide someone was intruding upon their territory.

All, of course, except for Randy, who liked his men rough, tough, and angry.

Thursday nights were important to each of

them, and they looked forward to it from Friday morning until the next gathering the following week. They also met on Halloween, and Christmas Eve. And one time, they met on Oscar night, just because they were trying to cast a spell that would make Angelina Jolie fall off the stage, thus freeing up Brad Pitt for the rest of their lives. The spell failed, of course, because two of the witches secretly wanted Brad Pitt to be the one to fall off the stage—not that they would have admitted this to the others, you understand. Although an argument could be made that, later in history, when Angie and Brad did ultimately divorce, that the spell might have had something to do with that particular outcome. But it would have been a really thin argument.

The other problem with the spell, and with every other spell they attempted to cast, was this: they were quite possibly the worst witches on the face of the planet. Except for Randy, but none of them, including Randy himself, knew this.

They had read all the books they could get their hands on concerning the craft of witching. Belinda, their leader, had read almost everything, which, in the eyes of the awed others, made her the leader. She'd read "The Necronomicon", albeit a paperback version. "The Devil's Handbook —The Illustrated Version", and "Good Omens"—which is where Randy had found most of his power that he wasn't aware of—were books she had made them all read. And there was "The Devil's Bible"—

three different versions, all downloaded from the internet, none of which were less than two hundred pages. When Belinda had run out of copy paper, she had grabbed the closest pile of papers possible, which consisted of three hundred and fifty lost kitty flyers she was supposed to have posted in her neighborhood and never did because she knew where the cat was, and a stack of newsletters she had printed for the PTA and forgot to take in that morning. She had also studied several biographies and texts she had purchased at a Wiccan store near "South of the Border" in South Carolina.

There were several spell books on the shelves of the office in the warehouse, but the most coveted one, the one upon which they prayed and revered above all others, was the tome that Mary had found at a thrift store on Main Street. It was bound in a strange substance (consistent arguments were favoring either pleather or sausage casing—it was actually human skin, but none of them, not even Randy, knew the truth of it), and gave step by step instructions for every spell imaginable. It started off with simple things: healing paper-cuts, healing the wings of dragonflies, the warding off of pests, such as mosquitos, flies, and neighbor's cats, and lust potions. A third of the way into the book, the spells became more complicated and more powerful. The witches were almost to the midway point of the treasured book, which, for a group of five inexperienced and terribly inept amateur witch wannabe's, was a dangerous place to be.

Instead of practicing the spells at which they had failed (every one thus far) until they got them right, they grew frustrated and impatient, and would usually skip ahead to the next one. This brought strains of protest from Daphne, the librarian of the group. She held a steadfast belief that caution was indubitably the best side on which to live, while Wendi, who was the one that introduced leather to the group and had about fifteen piercings too many(she had thirty-seven), liked to live on the edge. If there was going to be an argument about anything amongst the group, it was normally between these two. Wendi always won because Daphne always backed down. She feared confrontations of any sort; she would even pay someone's overdue book fines if they gave her a questioning look when she advised them of the total.

And in case you were wondering, Wendi thought the book was made of pleather, and Daphne was all about sausage casing. But if we are being honest, she thought the book was really bound with sheepskin condoms, but she was not about to tell the rest of the group how she knew what those felt like.

On one particular Thursday in July, when the city was muggy despite the breeze coming off the Atlantic, the humidity oppressive, and the moon was at its fullest, the coven convened—

almost reluctantly. They had been at Chapter Seventeen (titled "Nine Month Love Potions", or, as described in the small print at the bottom of the page, "Fertility Potions"—'cause everyone in this city knew he loved you just fine until that screaming, crying, constantly pooping baby popped out and ruined your vagina forever) for a month, and The Sisters were getting antsy.

It was Randy, paging through the book randomly, that came across the spell. He was idly flipping through the back-half of the over-sized tome when he came across one of the more descriptive illustrations in the book.

"Oh, my," he said, pausing in his perusing. Turning the book sideways, and then tilting his head in the other direction, he gasped. "Girls, when I get my vag, I am *so* doing *this*."

Wendi had just walked in and was hanging her leather cape by the office door. "What is it, Randal?" She was the only one of the group that referred to him by his given name, and it irked him to no end. Tonight, however, she did not get a rise out of him like she normally did.

He studied the picture for a moment, then shook his head. "I have not the slightest idea. But look at the look on girlfriend's face. Mmm *mmm*."

Wendi came up to his side and stopped short, her hand going to her mouth. Daphne was right behind her, and looked twice, before flipping her hand at it. "Seen it on the internet, looks too painful. Those women always look and sound like they're dying."

Wendi cleared her throat. "If I could die with that look on *my* face..."

"...I'd die a happy woman, man." Randy looked away from the book. "Even starin' at it too long is gettin' me all bothered. I mean, just look at her *face*."

Both women studied it. "Looks like she's having the best orgasm of her life," Wendi offered. "Color me jealous."

"It's obvious she's dying," offered Daphne. "That is a scream of pain."

Wendi laughed at her. "Daphne, you wouldn't know an orgasm if it was driving an ice cream truck and ran right into your clitoris."

"Would too!"

"Seriously, when's the last time you had one?"

"Like..." Here Daphne pretended to count on the fingers of her left hand. "...maybe...three weeks ago?"

"Are you asking me that or telling me? And was it with that Sybil girl at the library that you like?"

Daphne blushed. "I told you, I'm not a lesbian. That would be so stereotypical for a witch."

"You two gonna stand there and squabble all night, or you gonna let momma take a look?"

Belinda nudged Wendi aside and gasped when she saw what was on the page. "Is that..." She tried tilting her head the opposite way of the page, and her eyes got big. "Oh, my," she said.

"My exact words," said Randy.

"We are *so* doing *this*," Belinda whispered.

"My very own parrot," Randy said to Daphne, who was staring at their leader.

"We can't," she said.

"Of course we can." Belinda turned the book in her direction, pointing to the requirements of the spell. "We have enough people."

"But look at the picture! She's in pain!"

Belinda stared at her for a moment, then said, "I don't believe it."

"What?"

"You've never had an orgasm."

"I have too!" Daphne said, a bit too defensively, and a bit too quickly.

"Maybe it's that she hasn't seen herself or someone else having one," Wendi offered.

Daphne glanced at her, giving her a look that looked desperate and grateful. It was not often that either of them ever jumped to the other's defense, and the turn in the other's attitude was a tension reliever.

"Or maybe Sybil hasn't given her one yet," Wendi added, with a smirk.

Daphne glared at her, her momentary sense of sisterhood shattered. She really should have known better.

"Given her what?"

The group looked up as Mary closed the side door with a click and approached them, shaking off her leather coat. Beneath it, she wore a high necked, black satin blouse with a frilly lace collar. Of them all, she managed to still look stylish; everyone else was wearing tank tops or t-shirts.

"An orgasm," Belinda replied, and went back to reading the ingredients needed for the spell.

Mary set her big purse down on the long wooden table and stared openly at Daphne. "Your girlfriend still hasn't given you an orgasm?"

"I am not a lesbian!" Daphne yelled, then spun around and headed back in the direction of the office to get her leather vest. She was done, and she was going home. She wasn't sure why she kept coming anyways—they never accomplished anything, just wasted four hours of a Thursday night when she could be watching "Grey's Anatomy" or playing with the cat Belinda had given her.

"You know," Belinda said, almost to herself, "I think we have everything we need for this spell."

Randy gave her a good, long stare. "You think we're ready for this?"

"Yeah," Wendi added. "It's like, three-quarters of the way in the book, and we haven't gotten a single one to work yet. Not even that one that was supposed to make the cockroach dance."

"We made that roach hiss,' Belinda said, too defensively. "Everyone knows roaches don't hiss."

"The gromphadorhina portentosa does,"

said Daphne, standing in the doorway of the office, pulling on her vest.

"The what?" asked Mary. "And where are you going?"

"It's called the 'Madagascar hissing cockroach'. It hisses. And I'm leaving, because everyone here makes fun of me, and I could be home watching 'Charmed' or 'Buffy'. Or 'Grey's'."

Wendi approached her, treading carefully. "Honey, I'm not making fun of you. I just want you to come out of your shell."

She stopped a few feet short of her, and for the first time, felt bad about the ribbing they had been giving the librarian. "Look at Randy over there." Randy turned his head, an eyebrow raised in question. "You think it was easy for a young black man to come out of the closet like he has?"

"Uh, actually, I think you girls are the only ones that know," he said.

Wendi continued, unabated. "You think it was easy for a poor black kid, growing up in the projects—"

"I grew up in one of the suburbs on the east side of Cicaro."

"—to hide his sexual identity the way he had to? From all of his friends—"

"I had two friends in high school, both of them were gay. We just never talked about it."

"—to hide his true self from his parents—"

"They died when I was three, and I didn't know I was gay then."

Wendi glared at him, then looked back to Daphne, a concerned look on his face. "Daph, it doesn't matter what your sexuality is. We love you the way you are."

"And," Mary added, looking up from the book, "we need five. The spell calls for five. You can't go."

"In fact," Belinda said, "we need you in particular. The spell calls specifically for someone of your size."

Randy glanced at her but didn't say a word.

"My size? What is that supposed to mean?" Daphne sucked in her belly (she didn't have one because all she ever ate was salad and steamed vegetables, and she jogged every morning and still worked out to the Jane Fonda videos her grandmother had given her) and puffed up her chest.

"What dress size are you?"

"A four. But I always have to get a bigger top because of my boobs." This last bit she said with a blush, further cementing the idea in everyone's minds that she had never had an orgasm.

"Randy, what does this number right here say?"

He looked down; Belinda was pointing at one of the ingredients, which read "four toad's nails". He was no dummy, he knew what their leader was doing. Stepping up now meant she could rely on him when it came to crunch time, and Randy had always been a team player. "Four," he answered.

"Wendi is a nine, Mary is a—well, I don't think she's been a size four since junior high, I'm a double x, and Randy here—wrong size four. You, dear, are it. You have to be. You are the most important part of this spell.

"Now, go take off that vest, and the rest of your clothes, while we get everything ready."

Daphne nodded, turned to go back in the office, then turned back again. "Wait, what?"

Belinda was already reading off the ingredients, and Mary was busy pulling the appropriate bottles and canisters from the bookshelf on the south wall. She looked over. "Your clothes. I think you can leave your bra and panties on if you want."

"Oh," Daphne said, and slowly walked back into the office. She had never been naked or almost naked in front of that many people before, not even gym class in high school. She had always been self-conscious of her body; her father had told her early on that she needed to stop her breasts from growing any larger because that was all the boys would want her for. Her mother had told her to never get fat because then the boys would never want her, and she would die an old maid. She had a rather conflicted upbringing, and she had yet to have much if any confidence in herself.

Twenty minutes later, the girls and Randy had the spell ready. Randy, the artist of the coven, had drawn the circle around the altar that previously had been serving as the snack table. He always drew the circle per the instructions of the book, and occasionally, when the mood struck him, he would add an extra squiggle or two. He thought he did this to thwart them ever actually succeeding. Deep down, however, in his subconsciousness, the magic part of him made him add the extras. When the book was written several hundred years ago, the witch that had committed her knowledge to parchment had left a few key things out from each spell. A true witch, a woman or man in touch with the magic within, would know what to add without having to think about it, and most probably without even knowing anything was missing. Such was the case with Randy.

He just didn't know it.

(It should be noted that the author of said book, aptly named "Crazy Hazel", had no qualms about sharing her talents with the world. However, she also knew that if her book ever fell into the wrong hands—like, maybe, four bored ladies with not one iota of magic between them—bad things could happen. She could ill afford a lawsuit at the time; it would have resulted in her losing her cow, four chickens, a three-legged goat that answered to Sir Bullocks on account of his rather large testicles, and an angry pig. Besides her hut in the English countryside, these were all of her worldly possessions. So, Crazy Hazel had left a few things out, thus ensuring her safety, not to mention that of the world's, as well.)

Belinda surveyed everything, hands on her ample hips. "I do believe that's it," she said. She glanced around. "Where the hell is Daphne?"

The rest of them looked around, then they all stared at the office.

"I'm...scared," Daphne said from the darkness.

"Randy," their leader said, "will you be a doll and fetch Daphne?"

He nodded and headed back to the office.

"Does she think we're going to sacrifice her or something?" Mary asked. "She should know we would never do anything to hurt each other. Without written consent."

"Ten bucks says she's embarrassed to show us her bod," Wendi said.

Five minutes later, Randy led Daphne from the dark office, and into the light of the seventy-seven candles which surrounded the circle on the floor. To put it simply, the rest of the women were stunned speechless by her. She was truly a vision, and a small spark of jealousy ran through each of them. That jealousy was quickly quenched by a greater feeling of fellowship and sisterhood. For two of them, at least.

Belinda looked at her and thought, 'good for her.' Which was quickly followed by a rather derogatory word for females that won't be shared here. Although it started with the letter "b".

Mary thought, 'we have got to take her shopping—if I had boobs like that I'd be showing everyone.'

And Wendi, Daphne's greatest critic, could think of nothing more than wanting to see what lay beneath the underwear she had opted to leave on.

The undergarments were a frilly affair; black, with lace around the important parts. The bra was almost sheer, and while it held the contents well, the size and shape were quite apparent. When Randy gazed upon her, he was filled with lust, but not of the usual variety. He didn't want to do things to them, so much as he wanted them. On his own chest.

The panties...as she finally reached the others, this was something she was most concerned about. Had she known she was going to be parading around in front of the others tonight, she would have worn something else. She had several granny panties in the top drawer of her dresser that would have been more appropriate, but these were the ones she wore every Thursday night.

"What does the front say?"

Wendi stepped up and knelt before her, almost reverently. She smiled as she read them aloud. "'Hell's kitchen'. With an arrow, pointing down."

"Turn around, Daph," Randy urged. "You got nothin' to be ashamed of."

She did, and got laughs of joy from the others. The back of the black panties held the words: "Heaven's Gate", with a target instead of an arrow.

Mary was the first to stifle her giggles. “Daphne, you saucy minx.”

Wendi was inches away from her behind and caught a faint aroma of perfume. She blushed, and hid it by bolting upright, giving a surprised “oh!”, and scampered off to where the snacks had been moved to. It had suddenly occurred to her that her feelings toward the usually combative Daphne had suddenly made a turn for the worse, and she needed a distraction before she threw herself at the woman’s mercy. The last thing she needed was anyone here finding out she was a lesbian.

Belinda held her hand out to the half-naked and furiously blushing Daphne.

“I ordered them online, from that Bewitching Attire and Clothing Outlet website. They were on sale.”

“I think they are perfect,” Belinda said, patting her hand and leading her to the altar. “If they had them in my size, I’d order them myself.”

Wendi did her best to not notice as Daphne took her position upon the altar; the last thing she wanted to see was...

“Okay, to start, Daph, you need to spread your limbs out at right angles—perfect.”

Wendi groaned.

“Wendi, I’ll need you in the circle with me while the others stir and mix the ingredients in the cauldron.” Randy checked that the water was at a good boil, and did his best to not smirk at the word "cauldron"—their "cauldron" was a fondue pot on one of those single, plug-in burners that everyone had in college.

Wendi stepped into the circle, careful not to break the outer ring.

Belinda cleared her throat, and Wendi took that as a sign to stop staring at the supine body of the wonderfully built Daphne. When she cleared her throat again, Wendi looked over at her, annoyed that she had to look away from the wonderfully built Daphne. Belinda looked down at Wendi's hand and motioned with her head.

Wendi looked down and realized she was still holding the bag of Cheezy Kurls. "Oops," she said, and quickly stashed them under the altar, then brushed the fake-cheese dust off on her black leather pants. Belinda shook her head, then cleared her throat again, and raised her hands above Daphne.

Now, to relay the words of the chant would give the reader a crash course on a rather powerful spell. Needless to say, they will not be related to you here. The last thing the world needs is more... well, just trust me on this; it wouldn't be good.

While Belinda and Wendi chanted the words of the spell, Randy was busy over the "cauldron", stirring and calling for the ingredients, which Mary diligently provided. She kept glancing at the circle, the book, and Randy. Mary was the designated timekeeper of the group, and she rarely failed at her abilities to make sure everything was proceeding at the correct pace. She had her profession as a music teacher at the high school to thank. Timing was everything when it came to leading the student band, no matter how awful they all sounded. The wind section might blow everything off-key, but they blew it off-key and *on time*, dammit.

When the final ingredient had been added to the pot—dill weed, if you must know—she signaled Wendi. But Wendi wasn't looking at her like she was supposed to; it looked like she was staring at Daphne. She snapped her fingers, and when that didn't work, she clapped once, and rather loudly.

Wendi glanced at her, seemingly annoyed that she had to look away from the absolutely stunning Daphne. Then she caught on, and touched Belinda lightly on the elbow, signaling the two-minute mark. Belinda nodded once, the cadence of her voice never faltering. From Mary's viewpoint, everything so far was going marginally better than any other spell they had performed. Meaning no one had caught on fire or gotten a cramp.

Then Randy was pushing the chalice—a coffee mug with a picture of a muscular man in a white t-shirt on it—when the mug was hot, the t-shirt disappeared—into her hand, and Mary performed what should have been her last duty of the night: she walked to the circle, caught Wendi's attention again, and handed the potion over, careful not to disturb the circle on the floor. Then she retreated to the table and stood beside Randy, who was wiping his hands off on a towel.

Wendi held the chalice/racy mug out while Belinda began waving her hands over it, her chanting now imploring the Earth Mother and any otherworldly entities that might be present to heed their call and bless them with success. It was the same prayer they used every time, and it had never worked before.

That night, however, it did.

With the begging-chant complete, Wendi approached the altar and the awaiting Daphne. Their eyes locked for a moment, and it was Wendi who looked away first, her face filled with bashfulness and need. She was falling hard.

She held up Daphne's head and held the steaming mug up to her lips. As she drank, all Wendi could think about was how soft her hair felt, how her head felt cupped in her hands. And then she was staring down the length of Daphne's luscious bod, and her legs gave a quiver. All she could think about was sex.

And the cosmos answered.

Daphne began to glow. It started at her navel, and spread its way up and out, slowly but surely encompassing her entire body. Belinda and Wendi each took a step back, their mouths agape. This had never happened before. In all the years they had been practicing at practicing witchcraft, they had never gotten anything right.

They still hadn't, either. It could have been a combination of many things: some of the dust from the Cheeze Kurls, too much of a certain ingredient, that particular moment in time—any of these could have been a factor. But the one which sealed their fate that evening was one none of them had ever expected.

The glowing began to gather itself into one area of Daphne's body: right at the bottom of the arrow on the front of her panties. "Guys, this feels kinda weird," she muttered. She suddenly felt groggy, and full, like she had just eaten a big meal.

"Weird how?" Wendi asked, concern in her voice.

"Like...like I need to let something out. Like something is trying to..." She paused, her eyes rolled to the back of her head, and she moaned. Then her hips began to arch, and it took every ounce of control that Wendi possessed to not jump on top of her on the table in front of everyone and...well, suffice to say, her thoughts were dirty.

Randy squealed and clapped his hands excitedly. "Oh, let it out girl, let it out!"

Mary smiled, joy filling her heart. They had finally gotten one right! They could actually call themselves witches now! And most importantly, Daphne was finally having an orgasm!

Only, she wasn't. Her eyes came back into focus, and her brows met in a frown. "No, something is definitely trying to get out."

Belinda glanced down at the glowing area, and it was easy to see what was happening: something was sticking out down there. And that most certainly had not been in the picture.

"I think she's growing a penis," she heard herself say.

"Oh, God, no," said Wendi.

"Well that's not something you hear every day," Mary offered.

"I wanna see," Randy said.

"It's coming out!" Daphne was obviously in some discomfort; her writhing no longer looked sexual, and her face was growing tight with pain. "And it's not a frigging penis!"

Wendi sprang into action, rushing to the other side of the altar and grabbing one side of the panties. "Sorry, honey," she said, "but these have got to come off."

With that, she ripped first one side, then leaning over her, the other. To Wendi's credit, this was not done solely for the purpose of catching a glimpse of Daphne's privates—although she did, and she was and still is not ashamed. With the cloth torn away, they could all now see what exactly was going on down below, and it certainly was not a penis.

It was a small, four-fingered hand, no bigger than a baby's hand. But there the similarities ended: it was red and had long black fingernails.

"Oh sweet baby Jesus," intoned Randy.

"If that's a baby, it isn't Jesus," Mary answered.

As Wendi took a step back, shock and dismay contorting her features, Belinda took over. “Randy, what’s the name of that spell?”

“It’s smudged,” he said. “I need more light!”

Mary rushed to the far wall by the entrance and flicked the light switch. Harsh fluorescents kicked on overhead, bringing a harsh reality to the situation. Daphne was bathed in sweat, and the little hand was sticking out even further, the wrist out and flexing, feeling around as if trying to find something to grab onto.

“I think it says ‘daemon orgasmos’. Or ‘Damon's cosmos’. I think.”

“Daphne, you’re our Latin master, what’s it mean?”

Leaning up on her elbows, anger and pain blushing her cheeks, she gritted her teeth and growled back, “demon fucking orgasm, you assholes!”

“So...why is she pushing a little baby demon out of her vagina?” Wendi asked, perplexed, but also kind of fascinated.

“Randy, what are the warnings on the spell?”

“The usual,” he called back. For some reason, they were all yelling now, despite the lack of any other noise in the room. “Don’t break the circle, say the words exactly, do not add any unnecessary ingredients, no one but the object of the spell should be aroused, and something about no words expressing entries to our world or any other..."

They all looked at Daphne at the same time. Even Wendi, who was looking at her out of guilt. She knew she had broken one of the rules herself.

"Oh," Belinda said. "Shit. I think we turned her jay-jay into a portal to hell."

There was a moment of silence and inaction, as the realization crept in. Then Mary screamed, turned tail, and ran from the building.

The others stared after her.

"Well, FUCK!" yelled Daphne. "Will somebody freaking do something? I can't keep it in here much longer!"

Randy's face lit up. "Hey, if we got a demon to come outta her coochie, maybe we can get an angel to come outta her bootie! Let 'em fight it out!"

"Think," Wendi said, grabbing Belinda by the shoulders, and ignoring Randy. "What is the glowing crap inside of her?"

"I don't know, it's something immaterial, something like a gaseous state maybe? A spirit?"

Wendi knelt between Daphne's legs, peering into where the arm, which was now out past the elbow, was coming from. "I can't see anything past the arm, just the glow. I think it only gets a solid form as it comes out."

She looked at Belinda and shrugged. "I guess?"

"So stick that damn thing back up there!" Randy cried. "There's nothing in here about reversing the spell, so y'all better come up with something quick!" Then, to himself: "y'all shoulda just tried to pull an angel outta her ass."

"He's right," Belinda said. "Randy, find me something to shove it back in with."

He looked around, but all he saw was Mary's purse, left behind when the silly bitch had panicked. He emptied the contents upon the table and marveled at how much she had had in there. He spotted what they needed right away though. If anything was designed to tackle a Demon From the Baby Hole, this was it. He grabbed it and bounced around the table.

Wendi saw what he was holding, and her eyes grew wide with surprise. "She was carrying *that* in her *purse*?!"

Brandishing it above his head like a victorious warrior, the fluorescent lighting reflecting off of it in an almost holy haze, Randy totally forgot about the Heaven's Gate idea. This was so much better.

It was an eight-inch long black vibrator.

"Girl's got taste," Randy beamed.

"Randy, now!" Belinda yelled. Opting to not try and cover the distance between the table and the circle, he threw the vibrator to her. This, you realize, did not end well for the sex toy.

Randy had shied away from sports when he was a kid. Having lived with his aunt and uncle, who were born again Christians, and believed that all free time should be spent feeling guilty and punishing yourself, they had never enrolled him in little league, football, soccer—not even bowling. So to say that Randy's throw was horrible would be inaccurate.

It was, truly, the worst throw in the history of anyone throwing anything even vaguely phallic-shaped. The big black vibrator sailed off to the right of the circle and hit the wall with enough force to snap off the battery cap on the end. He cursed and ran to the broken member, and held up both pieces, the batteries spilling out and falling to the floor.

"I killed it!" he yelled. "Oh, Lord, I've killed us all!"

And Wendi, for the third time that evening, took control. In her mind, Randy breaking the fake Johnson had given her an idea. "Gimme!" she said, and this time he carefully handed it over the edge of the circle.

"Now, go find something to seal this thing with." Wendi turned to Daphne and gave her her best reassuring grin, which looked a bit lecherous. "Trust me on this one, Daph."

She leaned over, carefully studied the waving arm ('looks like it's waving hello,' she thought), and timed her attack. She placed the battery cap at the edge of the altar, sending a silent prayer to whoever was listening (no one was) that it didn't get kicked off. This whole process depended on timing and speed.

Wendi mentally counted to three, then slammed the open end of the vibrator home. The little demon arm fit perfectly inside the battery compartment. She pushed the vibrator right up to the "open portal" and held it there.

"Bee, help me hold it!"

Belinda crowded in and grabbed the end of it, holding it steady. It was thrumming slightly, and Wendi knew it was about to get a lot tougher to handle.

"Now Daphne, push!"

She nodded to Wendi, gripped the sides of the altar, screamed, and pushed her Kegel's as hard as she could. It took every ounce of muscle that Wendi and Belinda had to keep the vibrator from shooting across the room. Robbed of oxygen, the glow practically slammed its way into the rubber phallus.

"Randy, get in here!" Wendi cried, and motioned to where she had set the round, broken cap. He grabbed it, noting the crack which ran along the threads on the inside. As soon as she pulled the base of the vibrator away from Daphne's now vacant demon birth tunnel, he slipped it over the open end.

Wendi's hand replaced his, and he was then tearing off strips of the duct tape he had found in Mary's bag. She held onto the shaking vibrator with all of her might, every muscle in her body tense against the strain. She eased her hand down so the top of the cap was showing in her fist, and Wendi told her to lay it over her hand.

"Now grab the bottom and hold on tight," she said. Then Wendi let go with her other hand, and in one fluid motion, slammed the cap home and slid the duct tape over and around the cracked piece of plastic, her fist moving away at the same time.

It almost looked like when that archaeologist in that movie was swiping the idol with the bag of sand. Except the idol was now a big, black, vibrating rubber penis.

Randy kept handing her strips of duct tape, which she wrapped around and around the base. The demon inside seemed to be losing some of its fight, realizing it was trapped. The vibrator was glowing, but the shaking force seemed to be dissipating.

When the base was fully wrapped in the strong, gray tape, they set it on the floor and stared at it. Daphne sat up, breathing heavily. "I feel like I just gave birth."

Wendi smiled at her, then hugged her. "You were so brave," she said.

Daphne sagged in the other's arms. "I was scared," she whispered, and began to cry.

"We all were, baby," Randy said, leaning in to pat her on the back. "But you did well."

"I'm just glad you're okay." Belinda squeezed her shoulder. "As of tonight, I'm officially done with this witchcraft bullshit."

"Oh, shit, me too!" Randy glanced down at the still thrumming vibrator, which was bouncing lightly on the cement floor. "After tonight, I don't care if I never see another magic potion in my life. Shit got real."

Wendi laughed. "Yes, it did." She gently eased Daphne away, as much as she hated to. Belinda and Randy had picked up the vibrator and were both carrying it carefully over to the table. The glow was still strong, but the vibration was now very weak. Like the device was running low on batteries, only this time it was a blessing, not a me-time annoyance.

"Can I take you out for a drink?" Wendi asked her.

"Can I have some clothes?"

They smiled at each other, and acting on impulse, Daphne pulled Wendi in for a kiss. Although brief, it was the single most wonderful kiss of either of their lives. Their lips were parted slightly, their lips pressing gently against the corners of each other's mouths. There was no "swapping of spit" or "hockeying of the tonsils". It was a slight, caring, tingling kind of kiss.

When they broke apart, it took each of them a moment to gather themselves.

Wendi cleared her throat. "I thought you weren't a lesbian."

"I'm not," Daphne answered. "I'm bi."

"Oh, hell yeah," Wendi said, smiling from ear to ear as she went to the office to fetch her clothes. Of course, Belinda and Randy missed the entire proceedings, as they were each now holding a handle of Mary's discarded purse, the Vibrator from Hell humming within.

As they departed the warehouse for the last time, they were carrying the bag between them, and Daphne and Wendi were walking hand in hand.

* * *

When the four of them left the thrift store, having availed themselves of both the book and "The Devil's Dildo", as Randy had come to call it, they were not empty-handed. After all, it was a thrift store, and there were too many interesting things in there to not leave with something. Even if said thrift store was selling magical tomes and possessed dildos.

A week later, the first meeting of their Feng Shui Club was held in Randy's uncle's den. Because really, what could go wrong with Feng Shui?

THE FINE ART OF DYING

At that point, the death of Howard Scott was an absolute necessity. It was not something one would question, or ethically debate, or attempt to prove some morally righteous reason to allow him to be left alive.

It was more like an understanding. Like knowing you have to cook chicken before you attempt to eat it. Or knowing that you don't stick your hand in a fire unless you actually want to be burned. It was a base acceptance of a foregone fact, something as sure as the sun rising in the morning and the Bills never winning a Super Bowl.

By summer of that year, Howard Scott, an Englishman with sandy blond hair, a slight belly, and a perpetually clean-shaven face, had laid off forty-three people, resulting in three suicides, all of whom had left notes naming him specifically for their ultimate demise. And the next day he had hired forty-four to replace them. He had also verbally reprimanded several employees in the middle of five office meetings, cut salaries, purposely disabled eleven toilets in the building so that all of the women had to use the fourth-floor bathrooms (the only ones he'd had the time to set up tiny cameras in), and fired a dozen people that had been with the company for over a decade just because he claimed they smelled funny. In his defense—not that he is a defensible person, mind you—George Moriarty, one of those sacked due to questionable aromas, did smell a bit like old mayonnaise, but that was entirely his wife's fault.

You see, the problem was not a question of his mortality, but rather who was to be the executioner. Of course, there were several people up to the task, which was one of the issues—it needed to be only one person; otherwise, there was more of a chance of others being blamed. Of the five people gathered in the board room at Scott & Associates on Monday, December 17th, 2018, Bonnie Tatem had the strongest argument for being the triggerwoman.

At twenty-nine years old, she had worked exactly three other jobs in her lifetime, but had worked for Howard Scott the longest. She was an attractive woman from a good family, and had come to the city of Beacon Heights looking for a career. So leaving the company was not part of her plan.

The group had, during their endless bickering of who had it worse when it came to the injustices piled upon them by Howard Scott, created a flow chart to better illustrate the level of abuses and vileness heaped upon them by their employer. At the moment, Bonnie's column was taller on the chart than Frank Torres's. (And she was convinced that Frank had made up half of his issues in an effort to look better/worse than anyone else, an idea which was not untrue at all.) They all sat around the oversized oak table, its surface gleaming dully in the poor lighting. Greg Butanski had suggested they only turn on the table lamps in the room when they met, just in case there were corporate spies in the building next door, watching their every move and photographing the proceedings through cameras affixed with giant lenses.

"You sure it wasn't like a graze, or a bump?" Alice Parker asked. She was sitting across from Bonnie, and had been Howard Scott's secretary for three years before she was demoted to Marketing and Bonnie was "promoted" to her vacated position. As Scott only liked placing thin, attractive women in his front office, when Alice's baby bump began to show, he moved her out as quickly as he could. She did not blame Bonnie for any of this—if anything, she felt sorry for the poor girl. Being moved to Marketing meant she no longer had to suffer the man's eyes boring into her chest at every possible opportunity. (He had even gone so far as to call her into his office on occasion and "forget" what he was going to ask of her, which of course was a ploy just to stare at her boobs.)

Bonnie nodded absently, staring out the wall of windows which overlooked Beacon Heights Central Park. "Grabbed my entire right butt cheek. Held it there for a minute, not squeezing, just...cupping it." She looked at Alice, wondering if any of them knew how difficult it was to talk about that incident. It had happened two months ago in his private elevator, and was the precursor to these clandestine meetings. "He didn't squeeze it. That was the weird part. Most guys, when they cop a feel, they squeeze. Not Howard. He just...*held* it." She shook her head. "It was creepy."

"For how many floors?" Frank asked, leaning forward.

"What?"

"You guys were in his elevator. For how many floors was he grabbing your butt?" He looked sincerely interested, which both Bonnie and Alice thought was just as creepy as a man cupping your butt cheek. And the way he smoothed down his porn-star mustache with his thumb and forefinger did not make it any less creepy.

"I don't think that's pertinent," Tom McIntire said. He was sitting next to Bonnie—and had been for every meeting since the start. If you asked Tom who the prettiest woman at the company was, he would have told you "Bonnie Tatem" immediately, then would have blushed furiously and run for the nearest broom closet to hide in. Tom was, by all standards, a total geek, and someone like Bonnie would never go for a guy like him. He was in his early twenties, and had worked in the I.T. department of the company for seven months. It was he—sworn to secrecy by Howard Scott—who had placed the cameras in the seventh floor women's restrooms. The guilt of said action bothered him to no end, and there were times he would lie awake at night, his conscience nagging at him.

He was tall, wore the most ill-fitting clothing, and parted his dark hair on the left-hand side. Physically unattractive enough that Bonnie was way out of his league, he was content just to sit near her.

"It's important if we're looking at the scale," Frank said, indicating the flow chart. "If it was for the entire ride up, then yeah, bump her up a couple spots. But if it was only a floor or two, it could have been an accident."

"An accidental groping?" Alice said, anger flushing her cheeks. "How about I accidentally punch you on the dick, pervert?"

Greg sat up straight. "Please punch him," he said. "Anywhere."

Bonnie sighed. "Look, it was, like, ten seconds. Five or six floors maybe."

Tom reached over to pat her arm sympathetically, but she leaned forward and rested her elbows on the table. The sudden movement had him cowering back in his seat, like a rabbit spooked by an aggressive dog. "Let's get something clear," she said. "The longer we talk about it and don't do anything, the less likely we are to do it. We've been meeting once a week for the last month-and-a-half, and all we've done is argue about who should be the one to pull the damn trigger. I've been passed up for promotions, told to show more cleavage, fondled, and told to entertain clients with my 'feminine wiles'. I caught him taking pictures of me on the company retreat in Cancun last summer, and if I get one more email about meeting for 'drinks and a go' I'm just going to waltz into his office in broad daylight and bury a stapler in his face.

"We decide this thing tonight, because the tiny fucking Christmas bonus is the last straw."

Tom nodded. "I concur. We figure this out tonight, or we stop meeting."

Alice nodded, and Frank sighed. "Okay," he said. "Bonnie gets to do it. But I think we should all be there, just in case."

Bonnie glared at him. "Is this a 'she's a woman, she's weaker' kind of bullshit?"

Alice, who seemed rather eager to hit something, turned to Frank, who was sitting next to her. "Please tell me it is so I can kick your spleen."

"I'd kind of like to see that, too," Greg said.

"Oh, for crying out loud, no!" he answered.

"It's so that we can all see it done. You all may think half of my issues are made up"—actually, nearly two-thirds of them were—"but I want to see it done, too. Call it closure. Call it me wanting to see that prick getting his head blown off just outta spite. Whatever.

"I just want to see his eyes when he realizes it was us that did it to him."

A silence fell across the room, then Tom said, "Not trying to defend Torres over there, but I kinda want to see it, too. And just in case something goes wrong, I want to be there for you. If you need help."

Bonnie looked over at him, and he felt his face growing hot. "Not that you need h-help or anything," he said, looking anywhere but directly at her. "Just in case he fights back or has a bodyguard or something." He glanced up at her, but Bonnie was looking at him with one of her eyebrows raised, so he looked straight forward and out the windows, into the night beyond.

"The dork has a point," Alice said. "I vote we all go, but Bonnie gets to pull the trigger." She raised her hand; four other hands rose in the poorly lit room, and it was decided.

* * *

After another hour of deliberation, it was determined that the deed would be carried out on Monday of the following week.

Christmas Eve, to be precise.

Frank had a gun, which he advised Bonnie she would need to practice with before walking into Howard Scott's office "like that guy from the *Die Hard* movies, guns blazing and all that shit. Guns have a kick to them. You need to be ready."

Bonnie agreed—no need to go into this half-cocked, as it were. This had to go off without a hitch, and she was determined—not just for herself, but for all those who had suffered at the hands of a man who seemed to make it a hobby to avoid jail time and the wrath of God Himself—to exact justice upon Howard Scott once and for all.

"And," Greg had added, "it needs to look like a suicide. Or like the gun went off while he was cleaning it. And we should vacuum the room afterwards, to get up all of our hair and skin and evidence."

Since Greg was the resident expert on conspiracy theories, true crime investigations, and general paranoia, everyone deferred to his seemingly superior knowledge. The fact that he also believed in Bigfoot, Atlantis, and that the Baby Jesus was going to return to earth in a spaceship made out of the same type of foil used on Jiffy Pop Popcorn never occurred to any of them during these discussions.

They met over the weekend at a gun range on the outskirts of town. Greg Butanski showed up in a disguise—you know, just in case the corporate spies were lurking about. He and Alice showed no aptitude whatsoever when it came to firearms. The best shot was Tom McIntire, but he claimed it was from years of video gaming, and that he probably could not shoot someone in real life.

After a dozen shots, Bonnie looked at Frank and nodded. Her hand and arm were sore, but she only had to shoot Howard Scott once—she hoped—and she planned on being at close range when she did it. She was taking no chances. She and Frank were both fair shots—surprising in her case as she had never touched a gun prior to that day; sad where Frank was concerned as he had been shooting since he was fifteen and was only slightly better now than when he had started thirty years ago. And he went twice a month.

* * *

It was on December 24th, at 12:33 in the afternoon, that they gathered outside of Howard Scott's office. Bonnie had his lunch laid out on a silver platter (honestly, would anyone expect him to eat off of anything else?), the gun in her hand underneath the tray the platter sat upon.

She was nervous, but not so that one could tell. Her jaw was set, her resolve undeterred, her determination unflappable. "Remember, give it thirty seconds, then come in. And make sure one of you closes the damn door."

They all nodded, except for Greg—he was busy checking on their surroundings. There were several places where tiny cameras or microphones could be hidden, and he wanted to make sure he wouldn't be recognized. Which would explain the horrible fake mustache he had affixed to his face on the elevator ride up.

The pressure they all felt was something personal and unspeakable in each of them: Greg, paranoia levels at an all-time high, was worried about winding up in a Turkish prison; Frank was wondering how to file serial numbers off of guns—were there files specifically packaged for that purpose, where to purchase such a thing, and was it the kind ladies used on their nails—and whether or not it was too late to do so on his gun (The thought of reporting it stolen had occurred to him, but only when they had all stepped off of the elevator, so it was a bit late for that.); Tom was worried for Bonnie, and seriously hoped she would not lose sleep over the killing like he had when he had killed a nine-year-old opponent online playing the latest Star Wars game (The child's crying from his headset still rung in his ears, and that was months ago.); Alice was thinking of her son, and hoping that he never turned out to be a man that needed killing. (He did not—he grew up to be a successful stocks trader, married a woman who loved him dearly, and had three children with her.)

Bonnie's stress had nothing at all to do with guilt, second thoughts, or the moral repercussions of committing an act of murder. She was just worried about getting it right the first time. There was no doubt in her mind that she would be able to pull the trigger. This was her defining moment, when she stood up for everyone else who had to work under the man's oppressive regime, when she stood tall and righteous for all those who had suffered under his creeping hands and wandering eyes and evil management practices.

She looked around at all the others, and saw the same determination in their eyes. (Except for Greg, of course, who had an entire file back in his apartment on Turkish prisons and his theories that the CIA sent people there whom they wished to keep silent, and whose main concern was making sure he did not end up there at the end of the day.) Bonnie nodded at them once, then entered the office.

Howard Scott did not look up when she entered, but did say, "You are late with my lunch again." His desk was on the far side of the office, in which were several bookcases filled with books on laws in several different countries, two small tables holding antique lamps, and one other chair, which sat opposite his desk. It was a metal folding chair, and was entirely uncomfortable.

His desk was adorned with reports, except for the space taken up by one pad of paper, which he spent hours drawing boobs on. Bonnie set the tray down on top of it, and he glanced up sharply.

Standing right next to him, she leaned in close and whispered in his ear, "Take a good look, because these are the last ones you'll ever see."

She was wearing a blouse, of which she had undone the top two buttons in a move to distract him. It worked perfectly, as he hadn't seen her take the gun from under the tray when she had set it down. He did not even seem to notice now as she pressed the gun to his chest—his attention was entirely riveted by the view she afforded him.

The others filed into the room. Greg was the last one in, and forgot to close the door, until Alice elbowed him in the gut. That done, Bonnie turned her attention back to Howard Scott, who had finally noticed the hard, metallic object poking him in the nipple.

"This is for everyone you ever wronged, you evil bastard," she said.

He looked up from her breasts and into her eyes. "You're going to shoot me, then?"

She nodded, and cocked the gun.

"Right where your black little heart should be," she answered, and pulled the trigger. The loud report shocked them all—it was different at the gun range, when you were wearing head gear that protected your ears.

But what shocked them even more was when Howard Scott looked down at the smoking gun, then back up at Bonnie, a slight grin on his face, and said in his clear, precise British accent,

"Darling, I lost that sometime in the fourteenth century."

* * *

To put things a bit more into perspective—and to further illustrate the fact that Howard Scott was a most vile and heinous man—we should now take a look at his history.

Howard Scott, you see, was immortal, and had been alive for approximately 1,301 years. Give or take—he had lost count a long time ago. For him, it wasn't about how old you were so much as how much you could accomplish during that time. He had several hundred books in his private study at home detailing his exploits, all substantiated by proof of some form or other. He had been a very, very busy man during his time on this planet, and absolutely none of it was for the betterment of humankind.

In his lifetime(s), he was responsible for starting three separate wars, pillaging villages in thirty-three different countries, murdering a countless number of people (with absolutely no discretion when it came to age, gender, or nationality), spreading disease over nearly every continent (For some reason or other, he never could get to Australia, which he considered his only unfulfilled task.), was responsible for the disappearance of every living soul in the Roanoke Colony, and had run slave ships out of Africa for four decades just to build up his coffers. He had also caused an entire school's worth of children in South Dakota to get cancer specifically on their right earlobe. (At the time, he had been infatuated with the 'cauliflower ear' that professional boxers were known to suffer from.)

Those were the grandest and boldest of his atrocities. When he could not cause the destruction himself, he was there to offer the worst advice to the most powerful people just to see how much disorder and chaos could be wrought. He was present for the Battle of the Bulge, had encouraged General Custer to exterminate the American Indians, and had strongly urged the British to "show those bastards in America a lesson" in the early 1800s.

So when you consider the service that our five stalwart heroes were performing for the greater good, you should understand that, while their complaints may seem minimal in the face of all the death and destruction Howard Scott had caused or personally committed during his several centuries of life, the reasons they had were enough.

* * *

"Or it could have been in Croatia in the 1500s. Volatile time, that was. Lots of fighting."

They all looked at him, dumbfounded. First of all, Howard Scott wasn't dead. Bonnie had shot him at point blank range, right in the chest. Secondly, there was no blood. Not a drop. Lastly, and for some reason even more striking than the others, he was not screaming or complaining or protesting at all. He seemed rather matter-of-fact about it, and that was when Tom almost peed himself. The man just sat there, casually shifting his gaze between Bonnie's eyes and her boobs. Disconcerting and damn frightening, it was.

"At any rate, not the first time someone has tried killing me, and I'm sure it won't be the last. Apparently I'm not a very likeable person. Too much baggage."

Bonnie raised the gun and pointed it at his head.

"Bonnie, love, give it up. Here, have a look." He opened his shirt, showing behind the hole the bullet had made in the silk material, the hole in his chest. They all watched as the wound slowly closed.

"If you shoot my head, it's just going to irritate me. Honestly."

She smiled. "I'll take that chance," she said, and pulled the trigger again.

Another loud retort, and a hole appeared just to the right of Howard Scott's temple. He glared up at her. "Honestly, I am beginning to get irritated."

"Holy shitballs," Tom muttered.

"Are you some kind of vampire or something?" Alice asked.

"Ooo," Frank added, "if you are, can you bite me? Please?"

He pointed at Tom, said "Precisely," pointed at Alice and said "Not that I'm aware," and to Frank "Go bite yourself, you fekking pervo." He looked up at Bonnie. "Can I please eat my lunch now?"

She nodded and took a few steps back, flabbergasted. What were they going to do now? She watched as he took a bite of the steak hoagie and went back to his reports—all business as usual, as if he hadn't just been shot twice.

After a moment of chewing, he looked up at them. "Something else I can help you all with? Did you all come in to turn in your resignations, or did you forget what your jobs were?"

They looked at each other, and Greg stepped forward. "Uh...does this mean we aren't fired, sir?"

He stared at each of them for a moment. "As much as I don't like Frank, and as much as I abhor babies, Alice...you all still have jobs. You should go do them now."

They still stood there, staring at him incredulously. This was getting odder by the moment. After a few more bites of his sandwich, he looked up at them, dabbing at the corners of his mouth with a linen napkin. He rolled his eyes, grabbed the gun from Bonnie's hands, and pointed it at Greg.

"You were right about the Turkish prisons.

Hellish, really," he said, and fired.

Greg had enough time to say "Eek", then the right side of his face disappeared in an explosion of gore, and he fell dead to the floor, which was white shag carpeting. Tom wondered briefly what the cleaning bill would look like, then realized there was a man who wouldn't die in the room, and he now had a loaded gun.

That was when he peed himself.

He looked just in time to see Howard Scott turn the gun on himself; he pointed it under his chin, and grinned at them merrily. "Cheerio!" he cried, and fired the gun.

The top of his head blew off—or rather, pieces of it blew off.

Then he calmly handed the gun back to Bonnie, and began eating his hoagie again. When he leaned over the plate, they could see right into his head. His brain, large chunks of it missing, was clearly visible to them all.

"Oh, Sweet Jesus," Alice said, and promptly threw up all over the corpse of Greg Butanski.

"Fucking *cool*," Frank said.

Tom apparently had a large bladder.

Bonnie stared alternately between the gun in her shaking hands, Greg's unfortunate, puked-upon corpse, and the immortal asshole who was calmly eating his sandwich as if nothing at all horrible had just transpired. How had something as simple as murder become so damned complicated?

Howard Scott looked up at her, a string of cheese hanging from the corner of his mouth. She pointed at it, and he looked back at her, confused.

"You have a piece of cheese there," she said, then wondered—she was bordering on hysteria at this point—how she could sound so normal right then.

He swallowed, then said in a quite serious voice, "Bang on dog banana."

There was a moment of silence, then Tom asked, "I'm sorry, can he repeat that?"

"Froggy mouse ball," Howard replied.

"Apparently not," Alice muttered, doing her best to ignore the gaping hole in the top of his head. But then she noticed that while he was chewing his sandwich, some of it was falling out of the bottom of his jaw. She turned and threw up on poor dead Greg again.

"I read somewhere that blunt force trauma to the head can cause brain issues," Frank offered, to which Howard immediately pointed at him, smiling, and exclaimed "Teets on a dictionary!"

"Well, shit," Bonnie said.

"Wine bung cheese," Howard offered.

"So we have to wait for his brain to grow back before he starts making sense again?" Tom asked.

The immortal douchebag pounded on his desk in apparent anger. "Flag fart donkey buzz!" he yelled. "Dishbowl lice ream, crampy pants."

Frank gave a little giggle, then quickly muttered "Sorry, boss" and turned away, covering his mouth. He had forgotten all about the serial numbers on his gun, and was now wondering how much fun they could have with this at the office Christmas party next year.

"Look," Bonnie said, sitting on the edge of his large desk. "Not up my skirt, dickwad," she added, and kicked Howard's chair for good measure. His eyes immediately returned to her boobs, and she sighed.

"Blarney bag," he said, which she took as an apology.

"You can't die, and we can no longer live with you. Which doesn't mean we need to die, either, so don't go getting any ideas. You are a terrible person, and don't know squat about human compassion."

"Maybe he lost his humanity along the way," Tom said, and started to step forward. Then he remembered that he had peed himself twice already, and stepped back behind Frank.

"Yeah," Frank added. "Like this could be his second chance at doing things right."

Howard rolled his eyes. "Francine dickcake," he said sarcastically.

Bonnie shook her head. "I think his time for second chances passed by a long time ago."

"Probably when he lost his heart in Croatia," Tom said.

Alice noticed the wound beginning to close up on the top of Howard's head, but now there was a strip of pepper hanging from underneath his jaw, and she blew chunks all over Greg's body again.

"He just killed Greg, in case no one is keeping score," Bonnie said. "He's still a bastard. No chance of him having a change of heart tonight."

"Could we please stop mentioning body parts?" Alice asked, wiping her mouth. "I'm pretty sure I'm down to stomach acid now."

"So we either need another plan, or we need to just forget this all ever happened."

"Bush prang pixie pecan," Howard said, and took another bite of his sandwich.

* * *

The regrowth of Howard Scott's brain took another forty-five minutes. During that time, Frank retained his job by being mostly quiet, Alice dry heaved only once, and Tom managed not to pee himself for a third time.

Bonnie was still puzzling over their options, which included encasing their immortal boss in concrete, chopping off his head (that seemed to work in the vampire movies), sending him through a wood chipper, and dunking him in a vat of acid. And not necessarily in that order. While they waited, Tom went through all of the game endings he had survived through, but unless they could come up with a +15 Sword of Destruction, or a nuclear bomb, he was perplexed as to how to do away with Howard.

When Howard did finally say something (mostly) coherent, the four surviving members of the Kill Your Boss Club were surprised. After saying things like "pencil monkey" and "phone booby dispenser" for nearly an hour, Frank was still trying to figure out if what he was saying was nonsense or not.

"Listen," Howard said, leaning back from his desk. "There really is no easy solitude for you here."

"Solitude?" Tom asked.

"I said 'solution'," Howard snapped.

"Okay," Tom meekly replied, taking a step further behind the befuddled Frank.

"You all tried to canker me, it flogged, so now you're stuck with mink." He smiled at them ruefully, and gave Bonnie a wink. "It was a nice try though, Buggie. Haven't had that brazen an attack since Lingonberry."

Tom, who was almost completely hidden behind Frank, said, "Where's Lingonberry, exactly?"

"Who said anything about damn lingonberries, you twit? I said 'Laos'."

"Okay." Tom was now completely hidden behind Frank.

"We all want raises!" Alice cried.

Frank nodded, then pointed a finger at Howard. "Yeah, give us all raises or we'll keep coming back here every week—no, every *Monday*, and try killing you again. And you'll never see us coming."

Howard stared at him with a bored expression. "I'll never see you coming?"

"Nope," Frank answered, shaking his head, a determined grin on his face.

"On every Monday?"

"Nope," Frank said again, then stopped his head in mid-shake and thought about it for a moment.

"Alice and The Dumbass both have a point," Bonnie said. Howard looked up at her chest, and she sighed and pointed at her face. "We could keep trying this, and eventually, we might get it right. Or, give us what we want, and we'll leave you in peace. As opposed to leaving you *in pieces*, which is an option I've been considering."

Howard grinned at her. "I'll bet you have, love. I like the way your brain works. Shows determination, tenacity, and Barry Gibb."

Tom peeked out from behind Frank, then thought better of it and went back into hiding.

"As far as the raises go…three percent."

"Fifteen," Bonnie immediately responded.

Howard looked up at her, bemused. "Five."

She leaned forward, and his eyes immediately went to her cleavage. "Fifteen, or we'll be back twice a week."

Everyone in the room could hear him swallow. Tom marveled at the thought of being threatened by Bonnie's boobs, then decided that, after the spunk she had shown tonight, perhaps not, and disappeared behind Frank again.

Howard Scott leaned back, smiling, this time looking her in the eyes. "Think I misjudged you," he said.

Bonnie's expression changed not in the slightest. "Fifteen percent raises for us, you have to approve our vacation time, you buy a presents for Alice's son every holiday, and you never touch any of us ever again."

"No touching?" he asked, almost pleadingly.

"You even get close to me physically again and I'll see to it that you never die, but you'll be stuck in a cold, dark place until the world ends."

A heavy silence fell over the room. Tom was wondering if Bonnie had gone too far, Frank was trying to figure out how much fifteen percent was (He thought he had it, but he was way off the mark.), and Alice had tears welling in her eyes. The fact that Bonnie had included her family in the deal had left her speechless.

"Okay, here's what we're going to do. As my suckertary, you'll want to write this down, Bonnie." He paused. "Did I say 'secretary' or something else?"

Everyone was hanging on edge, so no one dared correct him.

"Alright then. Thirteen percent raises, vacations approved, presents for the brat but only on his damn bar mitzvah—"

"Birthday," Bonnie interjected. "Not Jewish."

He glared at her, then continued. "*Birthdays*, then. And no bloody touching. But you lot will have to do one additional thing for this great boon being laid before you.

"It has come to my attention during this long life of mine that a certain monotony creeps in on occasion. Tonight's 'festivities' have shown me something, have given me the idea that this unending life of mine could be so much more entertaining with a bit of...*action*, shall we say.

"Therefore, once a month, you must all try killing me again."

Howard Scott expected immediate silence as they pondered, but they all agreed wholeheartedly. (Except for Frank, who was now trying to figure out what thirteen percent was, and getting more confused by the second.) Tom was so excited he nearly peed himself again.

"Deal," Bonnie said. "I'll draft up the contracts tonight."

"Lovely," Howard replied. He pulled his chair back up to his desk and began perusing the reports again, picking off pieces of his brain and skull and lunch as he went.

Bonnie joined the others and, as they began to leave his office, having to step over the unfortunate corpse of Greg Butanski, Howard said, "One other thing, please." The group stopped and looked back at him.

"Tom, would you please hold Bonnie's bottom for me. No squeezing, just hold it for a few moments."

They exchanged glances for a moment, then Frank, all thoughts of thirteen percent gone from his head for the time being, said, "I'll do it."

Bonnie raised the gun, and Frank took a step back and immediately returned to his remedial math skills. She pointed it at Howard though, and smiled cheerfully at him.

"Hold this," she said, and fired. The bullet hit him right in the middle of his high forehead. His head snapped back, and much of his skull's contents blew all over the back of his chair and the big windows behind him.

Alice turned and puked all over Greg's lifeless form again, apparently having discovered an untapped food reserve. Tom...at this point you would think he wouldn't have to pee again for another two weeks. Frank clapped politely and said "Nice shot."

Howard Scott cleared his throat, grinned, and said, "Chinese daisy sex food."

"Exactly," Bonnie replied, and as they left the room, Alice tried closing the door, but Greg's arm had flopped into the doorway, and she wound up puking on the offending appendage.

* * *

When the door to his office had closed, Howard sighed, considering the mess which was Greg Butanski.

Then he shook his head and went back to his reports, humming "Holly Jolly Christmas" as he did so.

(Okay, he thought he was humming "Holly Jolly Christmas," but it was actually "A Boy Named Sue.")

SPACE COOKIES

First Mate Johannsen rolled out of his bunk, the Captain's voice a blaring contrast to the pleasant moans emitting from the dream-phones he had just been settling in with. The program involved three sisters from the planet Cardasian, and Johannsen was just getting comfortable with the volume controls when the gritty voice began barking at him.

He got to the com panel and pushed the appropriate button. The bastards that had engineered the ship had been pure sadists. They'd known the only way to get someone out of their bunk was to put the intercom system on the other side of the frigging room. "Cap'in?" he inquired.

"Get your ass up here, Johannsen! I got a fuckin' space emergency!"

Johannsen knew not to ask any questions over the com, as it would just garner a litany of insults and swear words from the man responsible for all of their lives as they hurtled through space ...

... although, as he thought about it, he noticed the ship seemed to not be moving. And, there were only two reasons the Captain would ever stop the ship. Seeing as how they were nowhere near any "whore ports," as the Captain would call them, that left only one thing.

A fuckin' space emergency.

* * *

They stared at the view-screen, Johannsen incredulous, the Captain furious, and Robot —well, he was sporting his typical expression. *"Robot"* was the name bequeathed to the ship's sole android by the Captain—the synthetic's actual name was Templeton, but the gruff leader of the crew had deemed the name ridiculous for something which "eats oil and shits computer chips." Robot/Templeton looked upon the scene with his usual detachment, which always resembled boredom. The First Mate often wondered if there was a programming glitch that got his "human" reactions all confused because sometimes he looked downright agitated when others were telling a joke or an amusing story.

"What the hell is it?" Johannsen asked, leaning in closer, as if the pixels of the screen would reveal anything more detailed than the picture they were getting from the four cameras on the bow.

"A fucking space emergency, apparently," Robot answered, the hint of a smile playing at the corners of his perfectly shaped lips.

"Goddam right," the Captain said. "Looks like a frigging cloud, but clouds don't exist in space, now, do they?"

He was right, it did appear to be a cloud. "Well, if we hadn't lost our Science Officer two ports back, we might have an answer—"

"For the last time, that wasn't my frigging fault, asshole."

Johannsen glanced at the Captain. "I wasn't suggesting that it was, sir. Just sayin'. . . ."

"Well, she ain't here. And one of us hasta go check that shit out."

Neither Robot nor the First Mate uttered a word. They both knew the Captain would hear nothing of going around it, which they probably couldn't do anyway. They were already close to having to use their fuel reserves, and a detour would burn through most of that, judging by the size of the "cloud". They had just enough to get to Ione, and would not have a drop of hydrogen left to spare.

Robot cleared his throat. This always gave Johannsen the giggles—he didn't breathe or eat, so what the hell would he be clearing out? Sometimes he felt the human behavior programs for the synths went too far. He had worked with one on a previous freighter that had constantly scratched at its non-existent balls. "Might I suggest we awaken Zod?"

The Captain tilted his head to the side, which he was apt to do when deep in thought. Once, the rest of the crew had, over a pot of homebrew, pondered the necessity of this. Several had been under the impression that he was a synthetic himself, and that there was a faulty connection between his mouth and his ass, which was surely where his main computer was housed.

"Just in case this… cloud, for lack of better words, is of a malicious nature. He is the only one capable of handling such a threat to the ship and its precious… *cargo*."

The Captain's head seemed to tilt even more. Johannsen could see the tendons standing out on the right side of his neck, straining to keep the giant mass of hair and mouth from toppling off completely. Johannsen squelched that thought as quickly as he could. No time for the giggles when there was a giant space cloud threatening their very existence.

"Someone wake up Security Officer Zod," the Captain finally barked, his head snapping up violently. "He's the only one who can handle this shit."

"Very good suggestion," Robot muttered, and headed off to awaken the "security officer".

* * *

"Security officer" was a loose term for "hired killer".

Seriously. Zod, another name bequeathed by the honorable Captain, was a big hulking man. He had specifically-modified genes that enhanced his musculature, his speed, and, for some unanswered reason —unless you asked Zod, of course—the size of his penis. In a moment of drunken honesty, Zod had informed Robot that he had asked for that particular enhancement as he was afraid they'd forget the most important muscle. He was proficient in several forms of combat, and had seasoned himself—voluntarily—on Ceres in the Occator Province during the OPEC Initiative, a bloody fight over the rights to mine and drill for the minerals and oils miles under the surface of the cold, dead planet.

Zod had brought his own ammunition and hardware aboard the ship, not something typically allowed by The Company, but the Captain tended to overlook certain regulations in favor of his personal well-being. Which was the same reason he gave for the on-ship prostitute he'd kept in his quarters for three months. The Company had not let *that one* slide.

So Zod, irritated at having been woken up, was in no mood for any fuckin' space emergencies. Johannsen and Robot had looked at each other with understanding nods as he grumbled and complained, then vowed to kick whatever space emergency ass he could in the next few minutes. After helping him into his bulky spacesuit and tucking the angry, genetically enhanced ass-kicker into the docking bay, they hurried up to the bridge, not wanting to miss a second of the oncoming galactic ass-kicking.

It was over by the time they got there.

* * *

They watched the replay on the screen for the eighth time, still incredulous.

Zod flew towards the cloud, the thrusters on the back of his suit hurtling him to his prey, his guns pointed forward, his voice screaming obscenities as he sped forth to victory and glory. He seemed to meet some resistance when he hit the cloud, slowing slightly as his suit encountered some type of membrane. Then he was through, swallowed up by the white, still fog. They could see flashes from his weapons as he began firing, still screaming obscenities into the void.

Five seconds later, the cloud spit out his guns and suit, and the helmet which still contained Zod's head. The video stopped when the head knocked into one of the lower, front cameras. The expression on his dead face was a mixture of irritation and surprise.

"Wait," Robot said. "Play it back again."

"Oh for fuck's sake, it ain't gonna end any differently!" The Captain yelled. "He's fuckin' dead!"

"No, not the entire thing, just the last fifteen seconds. To the moment when the cloud—er, 'fuckin' space emergency'—spits everything out."

Johannsen wound it back.

"Okay, play it back slowly... wait... there!"

The First Mate paused the playback as Robot rushed up to the screen. "See that, right there?" He was tracing a faint, curved line within the cloud.

"The hell is it?" the Captain asked.

"It looks like a tentacle or an arm, or some other type of limb. If you advance it frame-by-frame, you can see it moving. Like it threw those items out of the cloud!"

"Do it," the Captain said, scratching at his non-regulation beard.

Johannsen obeyed, and they both saw what Robot was talking about.

The Captain's head tilted again. "So," he said, drawing out the vowel. For a rather surprising length of time.

"What we have is a... a fucking space tentacle?"

Robot shrugged. "Something is living

in that cloud, and if the empty suit it flung out is any indication, it ate Zod."

"It ate Zod," the Captain repeated.

"Like a fuckin' space cookie," Robot replied.

Johannsen barely stifled another laugh. Definitely not the time.

"So if it is something livin', it can be killed, right?"

Robot nodded. "That would be the idea."

"Good." The Captain spun around in his chair. "Johannsen, go kill it."

Johannsen looked at him with a raised eyebrow. "May I speak freely?" The Captain nodded and waved at him. "Like, can I speak without fear of reprisal?"

The Captain looked at Robot with a raised eyebrow.

"It means he needs to say something important but does not want to get in trouble for saying it."

The Captain sighed. "We're all adults here. Speak your mind, Johannsen."

"Well, pardon my straightforwardness, Captain, but please go find a dark corner of the ship and go fuck yourself in it. Migs Johannsen is *not* a fucking space cookie."

"Yeah, I'm gonna have to write you up for that one."

"I'm just being realistic. You sent a weapons expert in there—an assassin, for God's sake—and he came out in pieces. What the hell makes you think I can do any better?"

"He is correct, Captain," Robot added. "You sent the one person we could rely on for the ship's defense to his death. All we have left is his locker, which, while filled with explosives and non-regulation firearms, has been left to a First Mate whose proficiency lies in running the ship, a synthetic who has been relegated to plumber and janitor, and a Captain who runs his crew with the hand of a bully and the brain of an incompetent teen-ager. No offense intended, of course."

"Don't make me shut you off, Tin Can," the Captain grumbled. "You're lucky I could only piece together part of what you said."

"Listen," Johannsen said. "Did we get any data from the suit before Zod got eaten?"

Robot leaned over a console. "Rudimentary data; temperature, humidity, oxygen levels, elemental composition... nothing on the lifeform, or forms, contained within."

"Maybe that's enough. If whatever that thing, or things, is living in is an oxygen-rich environment, it may be susceptible to the same conditions we are."

"Fuck me," the Captain groaned. "I got

rid of the frigging Science Officer because I couldn't understand anything she was saying, either. Don't push me, Johannsen."

"Captain, please. You are interrupting the competent people." Robot leaned back into the console and began running a scan. "The outer layer, as we saw, is penetrable, but manages to keep the interior contents housed nicely. The cloudy appearance of the atmosphere could be due to the heavy buildup of carbon monoxide over the years—it is rather warm and moist inside the cloud. Heavy atmosphere."

"But not toxic enough to kill whatever is inside," Johannsen muttered.

"Precisely," Robot answered.

The First Mate leaned back in his chair. "Obviously, it's hungry. If something eats, surely it also needs to drink."

"It probably has to shit, too," the Captain added, and nodded to himself as though this thought was the greatest one he would have that week.

Robot tapped his chin in thought. It made a dull thunking sound. "It probably obtains any moisture it needs from the atmosphere inside the cloud. Poisoning it won't help, and the ship would need to be decontaminated before reaching port, lest we inadvertently cause any humans who come into contact with the ship to be poisoned."

"I need a drink," the Captain said, rubbing at his temples. "You two figure this shit out. If that space cloud starts movin', alert me. I'll be in the bar."

* * *

"The Bar" was also the Captain's bunk, where he hid his non-regulation alcohol, and where he used to keep his female companion. That was, until the suits found out about her.

Easier to hide booze than it was to hide a woman anyways, so at least he still had that.

Pulling a bottle of whiskey from under his bed, he cursed his luck. It wasn't that he regretted ditching the Science Officer, although she had boobs. The Space Hooker had been a ready replacement. And there was no regret sending Zod to his doom without investigating the cloud further. The Captain's brain did not recognize, assimilate, or even understand the concept of guilt.

No, it was that, once again, the universe was working against him.

While he was a staunch believer in controlling one's destiny, it was, invariably, the destiny of others that always seemed to interfere. This frustrated him to no end. How dare the Science Officer speak with big words all the time, causing the Captain a headache-inducing mix of confusion and vertigo! How dare The Company look through the storage locker at the foot of his bed and find his pay-for-play girlfriend! It was the Science Officer's fault for not wanting to screw him, anyway! And, how dare a fucking space emergency eat his security officer like a fucking space cookie!

The freaking nerve of things.

He sat on the edge of his bunk, sighing dramatically to the empty room. Looking down at the bottle, he realized he still had a dozen of them left and needed to get rid of the evidence before they docked next week. Better start getting rid of it all...

* * *

Ninety minutes later found Johannsen pounding the console before him.

"There has to be a way around this frigging thing!"

Robot shook its head. "Again, we know not the size nor scope of this 'cloud', and thanks to that extra stop to 'drop off' our wayward Science Officer, we've not the fuel for maneuvering."

Johannsen sighed. An actual fucking space emergency, and the Captain was off getting drunk. Not that he had been any help yet, anyways.

"How long should we give him?" he asked Robot.

"The Captain? I should like to think until he drinks himself into a comatose state. But if he is going to be of any use to us and this... situation, we should stop him soon. Although, if his regular pattern of alcoholic behavior is any indication, we have another forty-five minutes until he becomes completely useless."

Robot smiled, and added, "As opposed to his usual state of mostly useless."

Johannsen, however, missed the latter part of the joke. He had a far off look in his eyes; an idea had begun to grow within his brain. A brilliant, exquisite idea. Robot had become a distant drone in the background.

"... moved in the slightest. Officer Johannsen, are you listening?"

"Hmm?" The First Officer looked over

at Robot, his brain still working out details.

"I was saying that since we arrived four hours ago, the cloud has not moved at all. Meaning however it got here, it just suddenly appeared. It has no inertia, no momentum to it. It is as if it were a stationary object, which does not account for the fact that it was not here when we passed through this quadrant ninety-seven Earth days ago.

"I suppose it is possible for it to have appeared from another dimension, but such a breach in the space-time continuum would have to be opened and sealed again, meaning it was placed here by a sentient being…"

Robot sighed; humans, despite being his creators, could be a fallow lot. "I've lost you again, haven't I?"

Johannsen looked back at Robot again, smiling. "Not at all. But I think we are going about this problem the wrong way. Looking at it scientifically is not getting us anywhere."

"And how else would you propose we address this issue?"

"The same way the Captain is. It's really our only solution."

"I'm not sure that I follow…"

Johannsen stood. "C'mon, Mr. Templeton. It's high time we raided the Captain's private stash."

* * *

“Ab-sho-loot-ly not,” the Captain protested. Although at this stage, the best protest he could mount was waving his free hand at his First Officer and his janitor/synthetic. Of course, he forgot which hand was free, and wound up waving his whiskey at them. It did nothing to improve the smell of the Captain’s quarters.

“I assure you, Captain, First Officer Johannsen’s logic is sound. It really is the only way to get past this... presence.” Robot peered about the cabin and decided that under the bed was too obvious a place to hide the contraband alcohol.

“Is my hooch! I ain’t sharin’ wif no friggin’ spaysh tenacles. Not hap-(hic), not hap-(hic), no fuggin’ way, *chief* (hic).”

“Captain, sir,” Johannsen said, getting on his knees so he was eye-level with the Captain, who had decided at some point that the best place to land was sitting up on the floor, within arm’s reach of his stash. “We cannot go around it. And we cannot go through it unless we know it is safe. Whatever killed Zod could be the size of this ship, and if that's the case, we're all dead. Besides, I think that being a company hero would mean a bigger bonus."

Robot nodded enthusiastically.

The Captain looked from one to the other. There seemed to be two Robots, so he was actually looking at three. It was a bit disconcerting.

"Bigger bonush?" he slurred.

"Bigger for you," Robot said.

"Smaller for us," Johannsen added, hoping the added insult to the crew was what the Captain needed to get him to the point of agreeing.

It was.

"Whadda I gotta do?"

* * *

"That is the strangest sight I have ever witnessed," Robot said.

Johannsen smiled. "It sure is pretty, isn't it?"

"I wouldn't say that. I mean, I've been a synthetic my entire life, which thus far exceeds two of your life spans. And this... this is the oddest damn thing."

Johannsen nodded. "It is odd, but if it saves us and the ship... well, I'll take odd over dead any day."

They watched as the Captain meandered his way towards the cloud. Behind him he was towing four kegs, all interconnected by tubes which Robot had told him would serve the same effect as a sprinkler system.

Robot saw Johannsen fingering the loop they had secured to the Captain's chest. "Remember, when you get in there, you pull this pin. It releases the valves and the beer starts flowing."

Of course, that wasn't the way Templeton had rigged it at all. But, even with the Captain as drunk as he was, he was not about to explain the physics of what he had actually constructed with twine and duct tape. The kegs would be noticed missing from the inventory of the cargo, but there were eighty-six other barrels, so the loss would be minimal when you considered the alternative.

Robot/Templeton pressed the com button. "Captain, please allow me to pilot the suit. We want you entering the cloud from the far end, not the center."

Of course, the Captain was nowhere near the center—he was actually headed in the direction which Robot wanted him to go, which was to the western side of the anomaly. But Johannsen had suggested the Captain would be insistent on steering himself, so all they could do was get him to do the opposite of what they were suggesting. This was a necessary issue, as the ship's logs and records would indicate that he took matters into his own hands and would not listen to the crew.

Humans could be so deviously smart.

"I know what the hell I'm friggin' doin', Spaysh Sprocket headed muvver fugger."

He looked over at Johannsen, who shrugged in reply.

A few moments later, they watched as the Captain bumped up against the cloud. *"Whadda fug?"* He bounced harmlessly off the cloud.

"Try increasing your speed, Captain."

"Doan you tell me, you friggin' GoBot!"

"What is with all of the 21st-century references?" Robot asked Johannsen. "Does he only watch children's shows?"

Johannsen chuckled. "Honestly, I had no clue that's where he was getting half this shit."

They watched the screens as the Captain increased his speed and bounced off of the cloud again. *"Muvver fuggin' bitch cloud!"* he yelled.

"Should we tell him to back up a click and try?"

Robot/Templeton shook his head. "It's far more fun to watch him bounce off of it, don't you think?"

The third time worked. He slammed into the membrane and, although he did noticeably slow, his entry into the western side of the cloud looked nearly effortless.

"What do you see, Captain?"

"Fuggin' froggy in here, can't she shit. Oh, wait, I can she the friggin' spaysh ten'acle. About the shize of our cargo hold. Looksh like it wants to shake hands."

"I sincerely hope I don't go to hell for this one," Johannsen muttered. "It's like picking on the stupid kid at aeronautics school." He leaned into the mic.

"Fugger'sh got me, Jeshush shave me, it's pullin' me—Oh fug ish got a big fuggin' mouth!"

"Captain, pull the chord now!" Johannsen yelled into the mic.

Robot looked at Johannsen as a tearing sound came from the speakers. Then a scream, a loud crunch, then silence.

"Well, shit," the First Mate said. "Guess

that's that."

Robot held up his hand. "Just wait."

They both stared at the screens. They could see a flicker of movement inside the cloud, then nothing.

Then there was a bright flash from within, and the cloud seemed to stretch and expand towards them. "He did it!" Johannsen yelled, and almost pulled Robot/Templeton in for a hug.

"Now, we give it a few moments. If this creature's metabolism is as fast as I think it is, it should be feeling the effects of the marinated Captain shortly."

The First Mate was grinning, then dropped to a serious expression. He cleared his throat and leaned back to the mic. "Captain, can you hear me?"

"You mean that wasn't part of the plan? Offer the creature the equivalent of a human rum cake and then over-intoxicate it?"

Johannsen shot a look at the android, then cleared his throat and spoke again into the mic. "Captain, can you hear me?"

There was silence, of course, as Robot expected. The ring the Captain had pulled was attached to four grenades from Zoc's locker, one for each keg. Not that the First Officer knew this, he was operating under the assumption that the Captain would be relatively safe from the blast. The plan being that the Captain would shove his payload away from him and towards the creature, the part of the plan Johannsen had devised. Johannsen figured that if the blast hadn't killed the thing, the alcohol being spread throughout its "atmosphere" would keep it intoxicated long enough for them to safely pass through.

Robot gave Johannsen a little nudge.

"Captain, are you there?"

Nothing but silence.

Robot went to the Nav Controls. "Let the record show that the Captain bravely sacrificed himself so that this ship, and its crew and cargo, could safely complete their journey."

He glanced over at Johannsen. "We should go now."

"Wait... did we just kill the Captain? You said he would get rid of the booze, pull the cord, and get out. That the cloud would contain the blast."

"As it did," Robot/Templeton replied. "Yet it appears the Captain failed to clear the blast radius in time. I will, of course, monitor for signs of his life as we pass through the cloud. But again, *Captain,* we really should be moving. There is no telling how long the alcohol will affect the creature."

The First Mate/acting Captain nodded slowly. "Okay. Please engage engines, full thrusters. Let's see if he was successful."

When the ship hit the barrier, there was no resistance at all. It was as though they were just passing through mist. Robot stared at the monitors and began to see glimpses of what remained of the Captain.

He hadn't made it.

Bits of cable, floating puddles of blood, and chunks of metal from the exploded kegs, all littered the eerie, quiet landscape. They also began to see chunks of flesh, but these were much larger than the Captain. Sections of tentacle bounced off the hull as they passed through the cloud. One of the outside cameras became covered with blood and gore, and the view on that screen added to the surreal sight of the floating gore zone they were traversing. Robot reached out and turned that camera off.

They were noticeably silent during the journey—even when they saw the creature in the distance, still alive, but having a difficult time navigating its way around. Johannsen zoomed one of the cameras in as much as he could, and the view on the screen showed a being with several eyes, which all seemed to cover its bulbous head. There were pieces of metal sticking from the torso, where its mouth appeared to be located. It was, indeed, a big mouth.

It looked like it was reaching for the ship with its remaining tentacles, but it appeared to be lopsided, and could not seem to get its bearings.

"I do believe it is intoxicated," Robot said.

The creature fell behind them and was soon out of range of the cameras. The cloud was all-encompassing, and it took another eight minutes for them to pass through it.

* * *

Johannsen stared at the screens the whole time. Sometimes, he thought he could detect movement in the distance. Always too far away to be sure, and never from the same direction the creature had been in. Possibly other creatures, but he could not be sure.

Then they were clear of the cloud. The unexpected appearance of the darkness of space made the First Mate jump. He checked the rear cameras and watched until the cloud disappeared behind them, soon indiscernible from the stars and planets which littered their vast stretch of space.

"We should arrive at the moon base on Ion in fifty-seven hours at this current rate of speed," Robot/Templeton announced. "We'll have to cut the engines on final approach, as our fuel reserves are about depleted."

Johannsen nodded. "I'll do the incident report."

Robot stared at him a moment. "Perhaps sleep would better serve you at this time, Captain Johannsen. It has been a rather long day, and I am quite sure The Company can wait for its report."

He thought about it only briefly, then gave the synthetic a tired smile. "Perhaps you're right, Templeton. If you need me, I'll be in my bunk." Even with all of the stress and death the day had wrought, he just wanted to get back to his dreamphones and planet Cardasian.

But when he reached the doorway, he paused and looked back at the only other remaining member of the crew. Templeton the Robot noticed his hesitation and turned to him. He smiled.

"You are no doubt wondering if this

could have gone any differently. If the correct decision was made, if the right person was sent. Perhaps you are curious as to my thoughts on our shared yet unspoken presumption that between you and the Captain, it had to have been him that went. Perhaps you are wondering if I should prescribe you something from Medbay to ease any unnecessary guilt or doubts you are experiencing. Perhaps—"

"Do you think he felt any pain? The Captain?"

Templeton opened his mouth to respond but he was interrupted by a blare of static from the com system.

"Somebody's gonna be in pain, they don't open the outer fuckin' cargo bay door!"

Johannsen and Templeton stared at each other, the surprise and shock plain on their faces. Then they were both scrambling for the controls, their hands knocking each other's out of the way in their haste.

"Space is really fucking cold, assholes!"

"You get to the cargo bay, I'll let him in," Templeton said.

"Right! I'll grab a medkit on the way down."

"I'll grab the medkit, you just make sure the Captain is calm enough to receive any medical attention he may need."

Johannsen didn't argue, and did not hesitate. He ran the whole way, foregoing the elevator and sliding down the railings of the stairwell. By the time he got there, the Captain was inside, and the oxygen level was stable in the large chamber.

The First Mate slapped the door release and rushed inside.

"Holy shit, Cap, we thought you were a goner!"

The Captain stood facing him, and indeed looked as though it had been a close call. There was a rip in the arm of his suit, his faceplate was cracked, and there was a combination of blood and scorch marks dirtying his suit.

He unlatched his helmet and tossed it to the side. "It was a frigging close one, that's for damn sure," he answered. "Freaking thing wouldn't let go'a me, even after the grenades blew off its friggin' tentacle. Ugly fucker. He's sushi now, though."

"Are you hurt?"

"Don't think so. But help me outta this fuckin' suit, it's hot as balls in this thing."

Johannsen approached him to do just that, but Templeton's voice from the doorway stopped him short.

"Stop there, Mr. Johannsen. Captain, please turn around."

The First Mate looked back at the android, who was carefully placing a medkit on the floor, then at the Captain. The Captain was glaring at Templeton. "What the fuck, Robot? You wanna make sure I didn't shit myself? 'Cause I assure you, other than having to piss like a Martian raceworm, my fuggin' bowels are just fine."

Then Johannsen noticed it, a small tentacle sliding over the shoulder of the Captain's suit.

"Oh, *fuck*," he said.

"Fuck what?" replied the Captain.

"Fuck your suit," Johannsen replied, and turned for the door.

"Fuck your own suit, douche-tard!" Then the Captain caught the motion out of the corner of his eye, looked down at his left shoulder, and screamed, "Oh, fuck this suit!" He began dancing around the cargo bay, slapping at his shoulder with one hand and trying to slap at his back with the other.

"Get it the fuck off'a me!"

"Captain, try not to aggravate it, there's no telling—"

"Go screw a light socket, tin can!"

Johannsen had made it to the door but

hesitated at the last second. He looked back in time to see the Captain ripping at the clasps and zippers which held the bulky suit in place, and thought briefly of the scientific ramifications of being able to present a living, unknown alien life-form to The Company.

The screamed obscenities from the Captain and the calm protests of the android became dull background noise to the thoughts playing out in his head. He saw himself presenting the creature to the Board of Directors. In his fantasy, it still had a hold of the Captain's suit but was securely encased in a clear, plastic box. No, no, better yet... to a panel of esteemed scientists, all applauding.

Okay, a panel of esteemed and rather rich scientists, all applauding his success while throwing credits at him. And all yelling "Bravo!", and "Holy fucking space cookies!", and "Can we touch it?". Oh, and one of the scientists was one of those incredibly hot blondes from the planet Cardasian...

Better yet, all three of the sisters from his dreamphones were there, and they were all clinging to him and looking up at him with adoration. And lust. And the Captain was there, crying in a corner... with a hairy, sweaty, naked fat guy that kept stroking his hair and saying, "There, there, my wittle rum cake."

Sometimes, Johannsen loved his imagination. He broke out of his daydream long enough to see a mountain of white flying at his face. The Captain's suit hit him squarely in the head, alien life-form and all.

Johannsen screamed and fell to the ground from the impact.

* * *

"Fuckin' thing almost had me!" the Captain proclaimed.

"Well, now it has your First Officer, Captain," Templeton responded.

They both gazed down at Johannsen; the alien had ripped through the suit and found some part of the First Officer's face, as droplets of blood began to fly out from under the ruined suit.

"Oh. Yeah. Shit."

The android sighed, shook his head, and walked to the writhing pile of human and spacesuit and creature, all of which was blocking the doorway.

"Where are you goin'?"

Templeton reached down and dragged Johannsen from the doorway by his feet, leaving a smear of blood across the floor. The creature was latched fully onto his head, and his struggles had become more intense. Johannsen's screams were barely audible, muffled by the weight on his face. It sounded more like someone screaming into a pillow. A sudden arc of blood shot out from underneath the suit, splashing across the floor in a wide spray.

"And so much for the First Officer," he muttered.

He straightened and proceeded to the doorway. Crunching sounds came from the mass of spacesuit and alien.

"Where the fuck you goin'?" the Captain yelled again.

Templeton looked back at his Captain, the human who had made his existence a living hell for the last eighteen trips aboard this ship. The human who had delegated him to cleaning toilets, vacuuming dust and dirt, and doing his laundry. The human that had ignored his extensive scientific, medical, astronomical, and aeronautical programming by insisting on having him assist in wiping his ass after every morning's bowel movement.

The android smiled. "Captain, it is best

that we contain the life-form for further scientific research, would you not agree?"

The Captain thought about it for a moment. "Is there money in that?"

"Perhaps," Templeton nodded.

"Then let's contain this fucker."

"My thoughts exactly."

He stepped through the door and pushed the "secure" button next to the doorway. It slid shut. The Captain stared at him through the small window.

"You motherfucker," he said.

Templeton pushed another button, and the locks engaged. Then he pressed the com button so the Captain could hear him clearly.

"The creatures are contained," he said, then turned and was gone from the Captain's view.

"Creatures? Creatures? *What the fuck was he talking about? Oh... shitballs!"* was all Templeton heard as he made his way down the corridor. Two specimens would do quite nicely.

BALANCING AFTER

The house, while looming above them with an air both malignant and indifferent, sat upon the crest of a hill, casting a long shadow upon the three figures standing at the gate. It seemed to care not about the world around it, and the oppressiveness of the structure was palpable. So much so that Graham Neil felt a sudden urge to swallow, as if the reflexive act would ground him not just to the moment, but to the reality outside the most haunted house in Newcastle.

"It seems a bit…off," offered Banks, idly thumbing the silver crucifix hanging from his neck. It was the sort of bauble Graham disapproved of; in his time as an investigator of the paranormal, he had learned that the dependence upon such religious or otherwise superstitious trinkets mattered not. There either was or was not, and if there were a God, he had yet to encounter Him in any shape or form. The same went for spirits, or anything of supernatural origin, a category in which he firmly placed all gods, Christian or otherwise.

Banks tucked the crucifix into his shirt; not because of any look or muttered annoyance from his employer. Rather, he had the unconscious desire to hide it from the house, as if it could harm the necklace in some way.

"Hence, Ophelia," Graham said, holding his hand outstretched to the open gate, bidding her enter first. While he had yet to encounter anything which could not be debunked, his staff always entered before he did. An agnostic to his core, there was no sense in him putting himself in harm's way if it could be avoided.

Ophelia Marsh was young, rich, attractive, but made untouchable by a scandal that had driven her from her native Scotland. Rumors had followed her, making her not so much a mystery in English society as much as it made her a pariah. She was welcomed in places but usually stood alone at social events and public occasions. Money bespoke her place, yet notoriety held her afar. Not that she seemed to care; her uncanny psychic abilities, which Graham always doubted as a unique mastery of common sense, set her apart from the common elite. She had always felt different, and therefore never felt put out or ostracized. It was how she preferred to be, as whenever engaged in conversation, things would come to her about the other person that would invariably slip out of her mouth. This caused no end of embarrassment—never for her, mind you, but always from the other party.

Ophelia regarded the gate with annoyance. Out of the three, she was the only one not impressed with the ominousness of the location, so her hesitation was borne out of irritation. How many times must she lead these horses to the trough?

"You want your divinin' rod t' go through first, eh?" she asked, eyeing their "leader" reproachfully.

He stared at her; four months ago, the same statement would have caused him to blush, or puff up his manly chest (she used that phrase as an interior anecdote—Graham's temper was quick, his tongue sharp, and his ego incurable, the combination of which making it prudent to avoid most confrontations with him) and launch into yet another tirade about the usefulness of order and obedience in such a small enterprise.

Lately, though, he'd tired of her attempts to goad him, and she was finding it more and more difficult to elicit an emotional reaction. This time was no different. "You could always go in the other direction," was his retort.

Ophelia gave him half a smile, turned to the gate, and stepped through. Two paces into the overgrown path which led to the house and she stopped, her arms half-raised, a slight tremor playing its way up her spine.

The two men glanced in each other's direction, and Banks was the only one to take a step forward to make sure she was okay. "Do not," Ophelia said sharply. He stopped immediately, not an inch from the waist-high, rotted gate. They watched her standing motionless for a moment. Banks could feel his heart pounding in his chest, and he looked about for signs of danger. Of course, there was only the house.

When at last she took a step forward, it seemed that the world began to breathe again. Graham sighed and let his shoulders relax, the tension rushing from him in an instant. He brushed past the still on-edge Banks, slipping through the gate and shaking his head. While the girl's theatrics could be a bit much, she was an effective medium—which to Graham meant she was a charlatan of no little exception.

* * *

The foyer was a small affair, large enough for a small coat closet, and a table upon which one could fit a photograph or a small vase. Anything more would have made the space cramped.

As to its present condition...old paint, peeling in long, jagged strips; the wood upon the walls which the paint seemed to be fleeing was warped, as though the English moisture had crept stealthily in and invaded the boards. The strangling moisture gave the wood a moldy and dying appearance, the life being choked from the architecture in a slow, meticulous fashion. The shadows on either side of the door were dark, and Graham wondered as to whether any light had ever fallen upon those black corners. The floor itself was bare, splintered in places. There were spaces between them, black and drafty. He fought the urge to peer closer into those little depthless slivers of night. Surely if the boards were to give way, they would fall into an endless dark devoid of all life and sound—besides, perhaps, for their screams...

He quickly strode past Ophelia, shaking off the vestiges of doom and proceeding into the open space of the hall. To the left was a sitting room, and on his right what would have been a dining area. Devoid of furniture, it was now just a larger version of the foyer. Depressing and overpowering, the open room seemed unwelcoming and even more claustrophobic than the front entrance.

He turned back to the other room; there was a dusty, purple couch set before the large front window, as if it were a theatre seat in which you could sit and witness the outside world passing by. In the far corner was a baby grand piano, propped up on the only unbroken leg beneath it. Canted so, and covered with dust and dirt, the white color looked more like bone. The ivory keys had long since been stolen, and some of the wires jutted from inside, angry remnants of its long-silenced voice. There was no elegance left to the instrument; now it was a sad, broken thing, like the house itself.

That was when Graham heard a child's voice from somewhere on the second floor. Ophelia had heard it, too; she was standing at the bottom of the stairs, staring up into the dimness that awaited them above. Banks was behind them both, still standing in the foyer. He had trembled slightly at the sound of the child, but neither of his companions had seen it. Which was good; his excitement was built of anticipation. Something stirred inside of him because he had a feeling of what was to come.

There was death in this house, and Banks felt a close association with death.

* * *

She led them past two closed doors and one open one. Graham stopped outside of the open room. Sunlight was slanting through a dirty window, and he could see motes of dust stirring in the air. There was a bed on the far side of the otherwise empty room. Its frame had long ago rusted and collapsed. The moldy mattress atop the splintered frame looked sad, its purpose long ago forgotten.

The sight of it stirred something within him. A child had been made here—perhaps the one whose voice he had thought he'd heard moments before. He was not sure how he knew that—common sense, perhaps. It was a bed, and beds were made for two purposes only, so it was no stretch of the imagination to think this is where the parents of the house had conceived.

But it rang such a realization of truth in him that he could feel emotion whirling within, as if he'd some personal connection to the room. He shuddered slightly.

"What do you see?" Ophelia was at his arm, looking at the muffled light coming in through the window. She had seen the look upon his face and had wondered, and not for the first time, if today would be different from all the others. Perhaps, on this day, he would finally see.

She glanced up at his face and saw his eyes

losing their moistness. A resolve built of steel seemed to creep back in.

"A broken bed and a window made of filth," he replied, the resolution and firmness of his voice sounding a bit forced. He looked down at her. "Nothing. Nothing is what I see."

She sighed, nodded once, and led the way onward.

* * *

Banks paused outside of the same room. His eyes went straight to the bed, never lighting upon the window. A twinge of jealousy narrowed his eyes, and a part of him longed to stretch out upon the bed which had once held two lovers, a husband, and a wife.

He shook off the thought suddenly, wondering why he should feel this way. Jealousy, and over dead people? Not his place, not his job, and most certainly not his requirement to feel any emotion towards any aspect of this job at all.

Then he thought of the other houses they had visited; had he not had the same type of reaction the other times, too? Barely perceptible, but still present. This thought he also shook off.

Better not to dwell in the past. Too much...too much...*something...*

Graham and Ophelia were at the last door, peering into the room beyond. Dirty, muted light was falling upon them from the windows inside the room. Even in the gloom, they looked a glorious pair. Banks thought they looked resplendent, almost ethereal.

He approached them reluctantly.

* * *

"Can you feel it yet?"

Graham glanced at Ophelia, irritation playing in his eyes. "I should think you know that I do not." Honestly, how she could still believe that he would ever be able to do what she did...

"I thought for sure this was the one." she muttered, finger tapping on her chin as she glanced back down the hallway. "We've been to all the other locations..."

She looked at him, the same look of expectation on her face that he had seen dozens of times before. He rolled his eyes, and she physically sighed, her shoulders rising slowly, then dropping dramatically. Then she cocked her head, looked into the room, then back at Graham.

"We go in," she said, and, grabbing his hand, led him into the room.

"What are you hoping to accomplish here? How many houses must we continue to traipse through before you give up on me being able to see your ghosts?"

They stopped just inside the room, and she glanced back at him. "Oh, these ghosts don't belong t' me," she responded. "And besides, ghosts are basically just mem'ries. Problem is that some o' 'em forget it, 'ave t' be reminded of such. Ye ken?"

Graham rolled his eyes at her. "How do you remind someone they're nothing more than a memory? That doesn't even make a whole lot of sense, Ophelia. Memories aren't visual."

"Not to everyone, they aren't. But to me..." She let that last bit trail off. She stared at him then, and he felt himself wavering under the stare. She looked at him this way when they were in the houses, usually in the rooms where she said "the terrible things" happened. It was all he could do to not step away from her when she did that—it was as though she were staring into his very soul. It was disconcerting, to say the least.

Then she was looking at their surroundings, and a slow smile tugged at the corners of her mouth. "This is it," she whispered. "You must see that."

He shook his head, but when he did, it seemed that the room shook with him; his perspective did not change, just shifted as his vision did, like his eyes were stuck staring down a tunnel.

"It's okay," she said to Graham. "I don't need you anymore."

Graham stared at her, bewildered. "Watch yourself, lass, or you'll be the one looking for work. It may be *I* who no longer needs *you*."

Ophelia sighed. She looked at Banks. "I'd prefer not to do it your way," she said.

"Not listening, is he?" Banks asked, glancing about.

"I'm right beside you, imbecile," Graham muttered. "Enough with the games."

"Graham Neil, look upon me," said Ophelia, and damn him if his entire body did not turn to her, as if being drawn by some unforeseen force. "It is time for you to leave me, and return."

"What..." He found the words escaping him, his urge to argue draining away as though it had been pulled from him like water dropped suddenly from a bucket. A cold chill etched its way up his spine; he knew this room. Just as he'd felt something when looking upon the broken bed, *he knew this room!*

"This is where you should be," she said

softly, but the words struck him like the pealing bells of a church. Images danced at the edge of his vision. This room. A different light, a different time.

"No," he whispered. "It isn't right..."

"This is where you must stay," she said, more firmly, and slightly louder than she had before. Her words ripped through him, and he suddenly felt petrified, affixed to the floor, unable to move, unable to protest besides a meek sound that escaped his lips.

"This is where you are meant to be."

Ophelia's voice was echoing in his head, although she spoke no louder than a conversational tone. He saw people walking about them that his partners did not see. Ghostly images, shadows, shades of the past.

I see them now, he said. But didn't say. Ophelia, whom he was sure would marvel at his admission of finally having sight, ignored his words, as if he's said nothing aloud. Which he may not have; reality was spinning about him in waves of history and flashes of now, rooting him at its center, cementing him as a witness, and as part of the structure. He could move no more than he could breathe.

Breathe.

When was the last time he'd pulled a

breath?

"This is your past, your present, your future. Move up and on, but never out and about. This..."

She moved her arms slowly around, indicating a small child, a girl, who danced past them, ringlets of hair bouncing on the shoulders of a white dress, her feet never touching the ground; to a woman on the other side, smiling down upon the happy child, her lips mouthing the words "slow down, little darling". Only he could hear those words in his head. He heard them ripped from the past and thrust upon his present, encompassing him...

"...is..."

...grounding him...

"...your..."

...welcoming him...

"...HOME."

A silence that Banks had not noticed before settled upon the house. He felt tension draining away, and saw Ophelia's eyes, cast downward, moisten.

He reached out to her, but she gave a quick shake of her head and otherwise stood motionless. Banks lowered his arm slowly. This was always the worst part for her, the letting go, leaving the spirit to settle in. He knew that for days afterward, she would be quiet and morose, until suddenly she would appear to him with a spring in her step and a light in her eyes which bespoke of another adventure.

He looked around at the room, seeing it as if for the first time. It looked to have once been the room of a child. There lay pieces of a broken hobby horse off to the side, cobwebs in the corners, and holes in the bare, crumbling walls. He knew better than to ask her what had happened here, knew not to press her for details. She would speak of it eventually, and if Banks was anything, he was patient. He just hoped the malaise would be quicker to dissipate this time around. The ghost of the man Ophelia had called "Graham" had stuck with them for months, much longer than the usual.

Then suddenly she was standing directly in his field of vision.

Her eyes, surprisingly, held a certain light to them. "You cannot feel them, can you?" she asked him.

He shook his head. "You know I never do. Can't feel 'em, can't see 'em."

She smiled wistfully, looking off to the side, her eyes following something unseen. "It is better for them that you don't, you know. They're all three t'gether again. Tis wonderful to see."

Banks shrugged. "Musta been a right nice family," he said. "Look, can we get out of here? I'm famished, haven't had a thing since..." He trailed off as her eyes came back to light on him. He really could not remember the last time he had eaten.

"I'm most happy that I didn't have to do things your way," she said, and then repeated the words. "*Your way.*"

He stared at her a moment, now concerned that something might have happened to her mind this time. It was always such a strain on her, bringing these spirits home. And lately, it all seemed to center around families.

"Your way," she said yet a third time, and now he saw no smile upon her face. "The shock of it would have been too much for them, and prob'ly for me, as well. At least this was the last one."

"My way?" he answered, taking a step back.

"Your way," she nodded. "Your final, killing way."

He stared at her, then past her. Saw the fresh paint on the wall, then the peeling plaster. Saw the fresh bedding on the tiny bed in the corner, then the dried, dark stains splattered about the empty space.

He looked down, and briefly saw the memory of blood, three people's worth, upon his hands.

"You never could see them for what they were, could ya? Not even in life, and especially not in their deaths."

She glanced about them, not just at the room, but at the history of the place. He caught a glimpse of brightness to his left, a flash of bouncing hair. It was gone just as quickly as he'd almost spied it.

"This is not your home," she said. "None of 'em were.

"Gilbert Banks," Ophelia said, "look upon me."

He did, and the horror of the past crashed down upon him.

"This is not your place."

In a split second, Banks felt the lives of this family before him, upon him, and within him. He felt the joy of revelation of blood, and in the next second, saw himself for what he truly was.

He could not recall his own ending, but he could that of those whom he had ended. There was such a mass confusion of guilt and exaltation and death and life. The full realization of it all threatened to buckle his knees. He knew what he'd been, what he was, and he saw now what he had never seen before: the true nature of his being.

"This is not your home," Ophelia said, and her words rung so true to him that his knees did give way. If only she'd understood, if only any of them had ever understood, perhaps then he would have been able to stop. All he'd ever wanted was a family, to be part of something more.

Then he realized that his knees never hit the floor. He was falling, straight down, and there was nothing to stop his descent.

She looked into his ghostly eyes one final time, and he could feel the damnation of a dozen spirits burning into him.

"And it sure as hell ain't your world."

* * *

To anyone that had seen Ophelia enter the house, they saw her leave the same way: alone.

Only this time, she did not appear to be talking to herself; she seemed to be singing. And there weren't so much words as there were sounds.

By the time she reached the cobbled street, she was skipping, and her blonde ringlets of hair were bouncing upon her shoulders.

A WORKOUT FOR THE AGES

"Where's Morty?"

Avery Hamilton looked over from his tenth attempt at getting into the Downward Dog position, which was thoroughly pissing him off. His view of Max "Rollie" Rollins was almost upside down, as he wasn't even trying to get into the position—the bastard was still sitting cross-legged like an old moron. Which pissed Avery off even more; these yoga classes had been his bright idea in the first place.

"It'll be fun," he'd said. "Besides, have you seen all the babes wearing those yoga pants? Do you know what we'll be feasting our eyes on every morning?" he'd said.

The only yoga pants worth looking at belonged to the instructor, and even that was a stretch. Literally. The class was populated by old women, and he dreaded the sight of the saggy butts and the cellulite every morning at seven.

Granted, at seventy-two, his old, black ass probably didn't look much better, but still—he could be home, watching those workout infomercials. Now *those* women knew how to wear yoga pants!

"I don't see him anywhere," Rollie said.

Avery grunted. "It's hard for me to see anyone with my ass sticking up in the air like this."

His friend looked over at him and grinned. "Your head's higher up than your ass is, Avery. That doesn't look like Downward Dog, looks more like Erect Depression Dog."

"And your face looks like Double Vagina Dog," he replied, trying to straighten his legs so his ass would get up higher than his head. The instructor, Anna, a woman in her late thirties, had told the class at the Shady Palms Retirement Villas Rec Hall that it was good for the lower back. So far, it had only served to make him feel like a jackass.

"I'm serious, Ave—he's missed three classes in a row. I haven't seen him since last week."

Giving up on the stupid dog, Avery lowered himself to his knees and glanced around the class. "Maybe he got stuck in the Crow pose and his tits smothered him."

Rollie shook his head. "He wasn't there for bingo on Monday, either."

"*Nobody* wants to be there for bingo. Fuckin' game is for old ladies and white people with no hope." Avery stretched, putting his hands behind his back and arching as far as he could. But, looking around, he didn't see their friend either. "If it'll make you feel any better, we'll drive over to his place after class and check on 'im. It's not like I'm doin' anything else today—besides the Sox game later."

Rollie gave him a grateful nod, and then leaned forward and immediately got into the Downward Dog. "Son of a bitch," Avery muttered, and made his eleventh attempt.

* * *

Avery's golf cart was the envy of every old man at Shady Palms—which, it should be noted, had absolutely no palms to speak of. There was a plastic one in the rental office, which didn't count due to it being fake.

The cart was sleek; it had a shiny black finish, a windshield, and cup holders. There was a compartment in the middle that served as a built-in cooler, and, after his grandson Marcus had tweaked the engine and increased the voltage from the six batteries under the backseat, he had once gotten that sucker up to thirty-four miles an hour. A few months ago, Marcus had gone so far as to equip the cart with what he referred to as a "boom box"; it was a portable stereo with two speakers on either side, and a cassette deck and radio and volume controls in the center.

"It's nineteen eighty-five, Pops," the young

man had stated. "And no respectable black man is going to go around in a ride like this without the most up-to-date and proper equipment." The stereo got shitty radio reception, but the tape deck played his Marvin Gaye cassettes just fine.

Every Christmas, he strung colored lights around the roof of the golf cart, and for three years had passed out candy canes during the holiday as he drove around the property. That activity had been banned last year after Avery had gotten particularly drunk one night and zipped from villa to villa, throwing the candy *at* people, yelling "Happy Hanukkah" as loudly as he could, and singing lewd songs about Mrs. Claus. Avery would go to his grave insisting that he couldn't recall any of that night, although he would lay awake some nights, giggling madly at the memory.

As Rollie rode next to him that morning, he smiled and waved at nearly every woman they passed. Avery shook his head in disgust.

"You know that half the women you're wavin' to are married, right?"

Rollie chuckled. "It's the nineteen eighties, Ave! It's all about open marriages these days, read it in the Cosmopolitan."

"Marriage ain't open when Crazy Charlie shows up with a shotgun," he responded. His reference pertained to a certain Charles Wannamaker, an eighty-six-year-old gentleman that, upon discovering his eighty-five-year-old wife in bed with a man fifteen years her junior last summer, had gone a bit off the deep end. He had retrieved his shotgun and proceeded to parade a naked Willy Jenkins around the community with three inches of the barrel firmly placed up Willy's backside. Crazy Charlie and his wife had been banned from the Villas, but you would still see Willy on occasion, walking around like he still had that shotgun jammed up his ass. Avery had spoken to him once about the incident over drinks at the onsite Moose Lodge. "Best thing that ever happened to me," he had told a shocked Avery. "All the women in this place looked at me like I was the victim, and, besides, they all got a good look at my johnson. Haven't spent a weekend alone since then!"

That conversation had reaffirmed his belief that good things only happen to jackasses, and that sex was getting damn dangerous. So he kept his eyes on the road while his friend peddled his wares.

"Yeah, there's that," Rollie replied. "Maybe that's what happened to him—he got caught with another man's wife and he's bleeding out on his bedroom floor!"

"If there was sex involved, the old bastard probably had a heart attack and is busy lettin' flies crawl all over him," Avery said. "And why does everything have to be about sex with you?"

"I'm in the prime of my life, Ave," Rollie stated. "You are too, you just don't know it."

Avery scoffed at him. "If this is my prime, my twenties musta been the weirdest dry spell in history. Besides, all these old ladies...ain't nothin' sexy about this retirement village, I tell you that."

The other man waved him off. "Tail is tail, Ave. Any woman willing is enough sexy for me. And you have an advantage, my colored friend."

Avery rolled his eyes, knowing what the man's response would be before he even asked the question. Yet decades of friendship had certain rules one adhered to, so he asked it anyway. "What's my advantage?"

His friend looked at him aghast, as though the answer was obvious. Which it was, but, rules and all. "Well, first off, you're black, which means you've got a giant schlong. Secondly—"

"Hey, Rollie?"

"Yeah, Ave?"

"Please shut the fuck up."

* * *

The outside of Morty's villa was quiet. The blinds were closed, and the men couldn't see inside. After several knocks on the door had gone unanswered, Avery decided to walk around and check the back door.

Finding it unlocked, he called around to Rollie and proceeded inside. It was dark and eerily silent. Morty was half deaf (a result of the war in Korea), and was one of the many residents that watched TV with the volume turned all the way up. Avery had tried watching a ball game with him once, and had made it ten minutes in before banishing himself to the porch where he could watch through the window—and still thought it was too freaking loud.

The back door opened onto the kitchen, and all looked normal. A few dishes in the sink, an open jar of jelly on the counter, no trash on the floor. There were two doors from the kitchen, one leading to the living room, the other to a short hallway that went back to his bedroom, the bathroom, and a closet. The setup in all of the villas was the same, but even knowing that, Avery felt no sense of familiarity whenever he was in someone else's home. Now he felt like an intruder more than ever, and a small part of him wondered where they would find his body. And how decomposed it would be. He had lost several friends over the years and was quite familiar with death. His own tour in the Second World War had also shown him enough of it, and on occasion, up close and personal. But something about the utter stillness of a corpse always creeped him out.

He glanced down the hallway but decided to check the living room first. There was no sign of the man there, either. The television was on, but the volume was turned down. As Rollie joined him, Avery pointed at the black-haired lady on the television. She was doing exercises.

"That's what I shoulda been looking at this morning, not trying to check out old ass from upside down."

Rollie shook his head. "Why is everything about sex with you?" he whispered with a grin, then started for the hallway.

"Fucker," Avery muttered, then stopped in his tracks. "Why the hell are we whispering?"

His friend looked back at him and shrugged.

They proceeded down the hallway together, peeking into the bathroom on their way past. Everything in there appeared to be normal as well, so it was on to the closed door of the bedroom. They stood in front of it for a moment, staring at each other.

"Do you think he's dead in there?" Rollie asked softly.

"Jesus, I hope not," Avery whispered. "The Sox are playing in two hours, and I don't wanna miss the game."

Rollie looked taken aback. "I knew you were selfish," he whispered, with anger clear in his hushed tone, "but I didn't think you were that much of an asshole."

He motioned to the door. "If Morty is dead, you think he'd care? He'd probably want me to catch the frigging game!"

Rollie shook his head, then reached for the door handle. Avery shook his head, then put his ear up against the door. The other man leaned in, doing the same thing. Besides not hearing a noise at all coming from the room, the one thing that he could detect quite clearly was the smell of the other man's breath.

"You taking that fish oil again?" he whispered.

Rollie nodded. "Why?"

Avery recoiled from the stench. "No reason," he coughed.

They pulled back from the door, and Rollie slowly turned the handle. The door pushed away from the frame with a creak, and Avery noticed that Rollie's hand was shaking slightly. Although he would never admit it to anyone, he felt the same way. This place was too quiet, too still, even for the home of an old person.

As the door swung open, both men took a deep breath, expecting the worse.

The smell assaulted them first; having never been known as having the most trustworthy of bladders, it was no surprise that the inside of the bedroom smelled like a portable toilet. Yet the sheer volume of the stench immediately sent them both to reeling. They stumbled away from the door, Avery's eyes watering and Rollie lunging for the bathroom so he could throw up in the toilet.

"Holy fuck," Avery uttered, and immediately regretted opening his mouth to speak—the smell was so bad that he could taste it at the back of his throat, and he was soon pushing Rollie out of the way so he could vomit in the toilet as well.

Just when Avery ran the back of his hand

over his lips, he heard Rollie heaving for a second time, and then he, too, was at it again. He managed to flush the toilet in mid puke, which made Rollie think to run the water in the bathtub he had just shared his breakfast with. They both stood there for a moment, panting, and then each used a different corner of the only towel hanging up in the bathroom to clean their mouths off.

Glancing towards the bedroom, Avery pulled open the medicine cabinet and sorted through the contents. Then he checked under the sink and found what he was looking for: a jar of Vick's. He unscrewed the cap, then applied a dollop to his upper lip.

"You look like a moron," Rollie said, then caught a whiff of the Vick's. "But good idea." He smeared some of the strong cream on his upper lip.

"And you look like a fucked up Hitler," Avery noted, then turned for the bedroom. "Stay close," he said, which was unnecessary, as Rollie was practically walking right up against him.

The smell was still bad, but not nearly as bad as it had been earlier. The Vick's was helping tremendously, even if it was making his eyes water. He pushed the door the rest of the way open, and that was when they saw Morty, sitting up on the bed and grinning at them madly.

"What the hell?" Avery said.

"He's gone off the deep end," Rollie said. "Time to call the men with the straight jackets."

Then Morty began babbling at them in what sounded like Spanish one second, then Italian the next. His eyes had rolled back in their sockets, and there were streamers of drool or bile hanging from his flapping lips. His head tilted back, further than either of them had ever seen anyone do before, and suddenly a stream of vomit spewed from his mouth and splattered across the ceiling as if it had been expelled from a canon.

"That's going to be a bitch to clean," Rollie observed.

Then Morty's head snapped back down and his eyes were boring holes into both men.

"Avery Cornelius Hamilton, your mother burns in Hell," he announced in a voice that did not sound at all like Morty. To Rollie, it sounded like a whole bunch of people all saying the same thing at the same time.

"Well, fuck," Avery stated, shaking his head.

"What?" Rollie asked.

"Morty's possessed."

"Oh," Rollie said, sounding relieved. "I thought he was going to be dead or some—wait, what?"

"Yeah," Avery said, and glanced back at Rollie. "And if he knows my mother, we're in a world of shit." He backed out of the room, pulling him with him.

"Let's go, buddy," he said, and shut the door. On the other side, Morty began cackling; it sounded like an evil laugh track to a sitcom.

"Where are we going, Ave? What the hell are we gonna do?"

"We're getting a crew together. Then we're gonna kick some ass."

* * *

Lou Miggs was the first stop—he was an ex-professional wrestler from the old days, and still worked out regularly. At sixty-seven years old, the black man, who'd gone by the wrestling moniker of "Nightshade" back in the eighties, gave definition to the term "aging gracefully". He was roughly the size of a small mountain, one that Avery figured they would need for the next few hours. And being the only other black man in the retirement community, he felt that together, they finally outnumbered the whites.

"You talkin' 'bout old Morty Banks?" he asked Avery, filling up his doorway with his monstrous bulk.

"The same," he replied. "Found 'im about half an hour ago."

"You sure it ain't roid rage? Lots of guys back in my day used ta get roid rage."

Avery eyed him. "You ever seen Morty? Does it look like he does steroids?"

Miggs tilted his head to the side and

thought about it. "Maybe he's coked up?"

"Oh, yeah," Rollie added, coming up from behind Avery. "Ms. Marrow, the old lady with the pink house up at the front? She sells all sorts of dope from her porch."

Avery shook his head. "She sells vitamins, jackass. And didn't I ask you to wait in the cart?" Turning back to Riggs, he said, "Man never did any drugs that I know of. Was always forgettin' to take his blood pressure pills, so I don't think he'd make a good candidate for Shady Palms Junkie of the Year."

Miggs studied him for a moment, his face serious. "We gonna need more help," he finally said. "Like, a priest."

At the same time, he and Avery both said: "Paulo Hernandez." They smiled at each other, and Miggs told him to pick him up after he retrieved Paulo. "Gimme a chance to put my house in order."

"Why'd you want me to wait in the cart?" Rollie asked when Avery climbed in and turned the key. He checked the voltage and was satisfied with the three-quarters charge. Although he had a feeling that his baby would be working overtime when it came to carting around a retired wrestler as well as three geriatrics.

"Because you always get all goo-goo eyed anytime we're around Miggs."

"Only 'cause he's famous!"

"Name one other person he ever wrestled.

No? Nothing? Then shut up and hold on Rollie, 'cause we gotta get to Father Paulo before he starts his siesta."

"Okay, but isn't this something you can take care of without getting the Catholics involved?"

"What the hell are you talkin' about, Rollie?"

"Well, don't you know voodoo?"

Avery turned his head and stared at the old man for so long that they nearly ran over an old woman that was walking three small dogs. Finally, he turned his eyes back to the road. "That is the most racist thing you ever said to me, Rollie —and that's the second one you laid on me today. I'm disappointed in you.

"Just because I'm black, you think I know voodoo, and I got a big dick. That's goddamn stereotyping, man."

Rollie looked taken aback. At last, he muttered an apology. "I'm sorry, Ave. Sometimes I don't think. And you know I'm not a bigot—we've been friends far too long for you to believe that.'

They rode in silence for a moment, and then Avery sighed. "I know you ain't. Just kinda tense and stressed out and all. Besides, voodoo won't help in this case."

Rollie glanced sharply at Avery and was about to call him out, but that was when they pulled up to the villa. But he was going to save that one for later; even if that train of thought had been inadvertently racist, he had been right—Avery had just admitted as much, hadn't he?

Ex-priest Father Paulo Luigi Hernandez—Spanish mother, Italian father—answered the door in his tidy whities, his olive skin and coarse patches of hair fully visible for the world to see. He listened to the men's story, then shook his head.

"He's not possessed. No such thing." He leaned close, which made Avery lean away—half-naked men put him off. "Maybe he got too mucha Meesus Marrow's cocaine, yes?"

He shook his head, exasperated. "She doesn't sell blow, she sells freaking supplements. And I know a frigging possession when I see one."

"Oh, well, you the voodoo expert, you be taking care of it," Paulo said, and stepped back into his villa, moving to shut the door.

Avery stepped up and put a hand on the door, stopping its progress. "I need a priest. You are the closest thing we have to that. You can put off your fucking siesta for a few hours. We have a man down, and I need a crew. These guys would do the same for you, you know. And if one more of you racist assbuckets tries to talk to me about voodoo again, I'm gonna make dolls for each of ya and start stickin' needles in the damn dicks."

Paulo studied him for a moment, then glanced at Rollie, who looked just as concerned as his friend and was nodding solemnly, his hands covering his crotch protectively. "All my years as a priest, I never seen no possessions. No real ones, anyway. Those people were just a bit loco."

"Well, no one's arguing that Morty has always been a few sandwiches short of a picnic, but right now, he needs our help." He looked past him, into the small house. "I'll even set up your VCR so you don't miss your soaps."

Paulo stared at him, then said, "You thinking it will take that long?"

Avery nodded.

"Because I cannot be missing 'All My Children'. Erika is in trouble, and Adam ain't helping."

"I have no fucking idea what you're talking about, but I'll set it up for you. Pronto."

Paulo gave him another serious look, then nodded once. "Set it up, I get my gear."

As he disappeared into the house, Rollie said, "I hope his gear involves clothing."

* * *

Once they picked up Miggs, they were the talk of the retirement community. Four men, barreling down the streets (okay, they weren't actually barreling anywhere—the added weight was slowing the cart down to about ten miles an hour) in a tricked out golf cart. To compensate for Miggs' bulk, Paulo was sitting on Rollie's lap directly behind Avery, and there was still a decided lean to the right.

They all wore the faces of determined and quite serious retirees, men on a mission. Men with a plan, and with a distinct air of righteousness in their hardened, steely eyes.

"What's the plan, Ave?" Rollie asked, trying to shift in his seat but unable to, due to the hundred-and-fifty pound man on his lap.

"We'll figure that out when we get there," he said, passing the street that would have taken him to Morty's house.

"We makin' a pit stop first?" Miggs asked.

Avery nodded. "One more thing to get," he muttered and steered towards the front of the neighborhood. There was only one thing he could think of that would settle Morty down enough for them to perform whatever ritual Paulo needed to do.

He pulled up in front of the pink house, and turned and looked at each man in turn. "Not a word," he said, and then went up to Ms. Marrow's door.

The three watched from the cart. Watched as the old woman answered her door, watched them talk briefly. When Avery pointed back to the cart, all three smiled and waved to her. There were more words, which the men couldn't hear, then she stepped aside and allowed Avery inside.

"He better not be in there gettin' some tail," Miggs said.

"He's here for the cocaine," Paulo offered.

"They put cocaine in vitamins now?" Rollie asked.

The men waited patiently. They could hear raised voices from inside the villa, but could not make any of the words out. "What do you think they're fighting about in there?" Rollie asked.

"The size of his dong," Miggs replied, which set the other two off in a fit of laughter.

Then all was quiet, and after another moment, Avery came out of the house with Ms. Marrow in tow. She had a handbag in one hand, and a large plastic bag in another. As they approached, Miggs tipped an imaginary hat to the woman.

"Morning, Mister Miggs," she said, giving him a big smile. She was wearing a long, flower print housecoat and had her hair up in rollers. Ms. Marrow was a handsome woman, one of the better looking of the women that called the retirement community their home. In her mid-sixties, she still had patches of black in her gray hair that sometimes made her resemble a reverse Bride of Frankenstein—not that any of the men would ever say so aloud. They all considered her a looker, and weren't about to insult a looker. She handed him the garbage bag and looked at him seriously. "Break this, and I'll break you."

The smile dropped from his face as he gingerly took the bag from her. "Is this Megatoke?" he asked, his eyes wide.

Ms. Marrow nodded. "You protect it," she said, climbing into the open seat behind him.

"With my life," he replied reverently.

Avery started up the cart and pulled away from her house.

"Ms. Marrow," Paulo said. "How are you thees morning?"

"Just fine, thank you," she said. "Ready to kick some demon ass."

Rollie swallowed. "Is that what we're dealing with? An actual demon?"

Paulo nodded. "If he's possessed, that's what's got 'im."

From the driver's seat, Avery said, "What'd you think he was possessed with?"

Rollie shrugged. "I don't know. Just didn't think about it is all. Anyways, don't you think this'll be a little dangerous for a lady, Ave?"

"That's what I friggin' said," Avery replied.

"Don't give me any of your chivalry bullshit, oldtimer," Ms. Marrow said. "You need me, and you know it."

"So long as I don't have to listen to any women's lib crap," he snapped back.

"Just drive, Avery. You can get us there without anything *breaking*, right?"

"Wasn't my fault, you old bag!"

"Well if you knew how to put one on properly, never would've had that little accident, would we have?"

"How many times do I gotta tell you—" He cut himself off, and looked at the other men, who were all listening to the exchange with rapt attention. “Just leave it,” he muttered.

Ms. Marrow smiled and clutched her handbag to her big bosom.

Paulo and Miggs looked at each other, and Miggs said, “Told you what they was fightin’ about.”

* * *

All was quiet from within Morty’s villa when they pulled up ten minutes later.

They stood out front eyeing it speculatively—except for Miggs, who was busy cradling the bag with a look of reverence. An old couple walked past, looking at them distrustfully. Avery couldn’t blame them, really—the group consisted of an angry looking old black man, a retired black wrestler, a Hispanic priest in full garb, an old woman with her hair in curlers, and…well, Rollie, who on the best of days looked like he had been riding railcars his entire life.

“Let’s get inside before we draw a crowd,” Avery said and led them around back. Holding the door open for them, he returned the wave of Mitch Blaggins, who was watering his small back yard.

“Everything okay over there?” Mitch asked.

“Morty’s possessed,” Rollie said to him as he walked past Avery. “Doin’ a little exorcism.”

Mitch looked taken aback, so Avery gave

him one of his winning smiles. "Nothing to worry about, buddy. Just helpin' out a friend."

"You still throwing candy canes at people?"

"Be on your porch on Christmas Eve and find out, you old bastard," Avery replied, still smiling, and pulled the door closed behind him. "Fucker," he muttered.

The others were waiting for him in the hall outside of Morty's bedroom. The sound of babbling and the stench of human feces greeted them, but Rollie was passing around the jar of Vick's. When they were ready, Avery looked at each one in turn, pointing at Miggs—who had ducked into the bathroom, because there was no room in the hallway with him in it—first.

"You go in first, and hold him down while Rollie and I tie him up. Father Paulo, you get your stuff ready." He turned to Ms. Marrow. "And the sooner you do your thing, the better. It's bound to get messier than it already is in there, and I want Morty as copacetic as possible."

"Kinda sexy when you use big words, cowboy," she replied.

"Yeah, I'll buy you a dictionary later so you can keep up." Before she could reply, he pulled her and Paulo out of the way so Miggs could get in first, then turned the knob and pushed the door open.

Miggs danced around him and Rollie and rushed into the room, his muscles shining and rippling. And promptly fell to his knees when the smell hit him full force.

"Holy shit!" he cried, and then instantly regretted opening his mouth. "Oh, I can taste it," he groaned. Morty was sitting cross-legged on the bed, grinning at them.

Avery helped him to his feet, and they backed up to the door. "Don't know if I can do this, man," Miggs said. He was shaking, and looked like he was ready to bolt.

"Pull yourself together," Avery growled. "This man needs you."

"It's the smell, I just can't."

"You better!" Avery yelled at him. "It's time to nut up or shut up, Nightshade! That man needs you, we all need you!"

Miggs looked at him, nodded, then screwed his face up in the look of determination and rage that Avery recalled seeing him do in the ring ten or so years ago. He watched as the big man rushed forward again, this time hitting Morty right in the chest with his beefy forearm. Morty flopped back on the bed, and Avery and Rollie ran over and began securing his wrists and legs to the bedposts. When he began kicking, Miggs threw a leg over his so they could tie the ankles as well.

After a few moments of struggling, cursing in several different languages and voices, Morty suddenly calmed down. He smiled up at them wickedly, his yellowed teeth a dull dash of color in a wretched, contorted mask. Avery and Rollie stepped back, and Ms. Marrow came forward, holding the biggest bong in South Florida in her wrinkled hands. "Plug his nose, boys," she said.

Avery secured his head, and Rollie clamped a hand over Morty's mouth and nose. She lit up the bong known affectionately as "Megatoke", and they could all hear the water bubbling in it as she took a long pull. They watched the smoke gathering within it, and just before it reached her lips, she pulled away and stuck her hand over the top of it. Morty watched this process with just as much attention as the others did; the bong itself was about three feet in length, and she had had to stretch her arm all the way out to reach the tiny bowl that held the weed.

"Tilt his head up," she told them, and Avery did as he was told. "Now keep his nose closed," she told Rollie as she leaned in, tilting the bong towards the supine man's face. When she was close enough, she nodded to Rollie, and he took his hand away just as she pushed the wide, open mouth of the bong around his lips.

Morty held out for as long as he could, but his face was beginning to turn purple, and finally, his lips parted and he sucked in a lungful of the smoke. Ms. Marrow took the bong away, and Rollie put his hand back over the man's mouth.

"Give it a bit," she said. Morty was staring up at her hatefully, but as soon as she saw his eyes begin to soften, she told Rollie to move away. Both he and Avery stepped back, and Morty exhaled, a deep cough rattling his chest as he did so.

"How are you feeling, Morty?" Ms. Marrow

asked him.

"Like how the inside of a college dorm in the sixties must've felt like," he replied with a lazy smile. Now, his voice carried out on an English accent, which grated on Avery's nerves. He didn't hate English people, but the ones with those nasally voices rattled him. It was like nails on a chalkboard.

"Perfect," she said. Looking at Avery, she told him she'd be in the living room. "You boys need me again, just call."

"Maybe I should go with her?" Miggs asked, and began following her out, his eyes never leaving the bong.

Avery nodded. "Just don't go gettin' all fucked up now, y' hear?" He turned his attention back to Morty, who was grinning up at them stupidly.

"Anybody got any pretzels? I could really go for some pretzels."

* * *

Paulo stood at the foot of the bed. He had been reading parts of the bible for the last twenty minutes, and it didn't seem to be having any effect on Morty at all.

"You sure you're usin' that thing right?" Avery asked in exasperation. "We're gonna miss the damn game."

"The problem isn't the book," Morty announced. He didn't sound as stoned as he had been a little while ago, but he still seemed complacent, so Avery had decided to wait on calling Ms. Marrow back in. Especially since Morty had kept asking for another hit on the bong—no need to give the demon asshole what it wanted. "It's his faith. He doesn't believe enough for this to work."

Rollie looked over at Paulo. "Is that the truth?"

"Listen, man," Paulo said, his stance becoming defensive. "I told you all before not to talk to thees fuck—er, demon. He's just gonna get inside your head."

"Right," Avery said. "Paulo, go take a time out. And find the part in the bible with all that 'Christ compels you' crap like what they said in 'The Exorcist'. That shit worked."

Paulo stepped over to the only chair in the room, which was in a corner under the room's only window. He was muttering something, and it didn't sound like anything a proper Christian would be saying.

Avery and Rollie studied Morty for a few moments. "What should we do with him, Ave? It isn't like we can leave him like this, and I can't think of anyone to call."

"Me neither," Avery replied, and ran a hand over his bald scalp.

"You want to talk to your mother?" Morty

asked him. "Oh, wait, I'm supposed to be insulting you."

Rollie stared at the restrained man in confusion. "Do you know what you're doing? I mean, it doesn't sound like you've been doing this for a long time. Possessing people, I mean."

Morty blushed. "It's me second time, actually."

"How'd the first one go?" Rollie asked.

Morty's face twisted in that vile grin and he giggled. "He's burning in Hell!" he announced. It was obvious that he'd tried to make his voice sound like that evil chorus they'd heard earlier, but all he did was make himself sound like a creepy Englishman.

"Rollie's got a point," Avery said. "Doesn't sound like you're any good at this shit."

"Your mother sucks dicks in Hell!" Morty yelled, his head turning in Avery's direction. "She drowns in a lake of sperm!"

Avery looked confused. "So...is she sucking dicks or drowning? I don't think you can do both at the same time. Can you?" he asked, turning to Rollie.

"How the hell would I know?" he asked, sounding a bit too defensive.

Avery held up his hands. "Hey, man, just a question. I ain't implying anything."

"YOUR MOTHER IS A WHORE IN HELL!" the Morty-demon roared, it's voice deafening. The windows rattled at the sound, and Paulo cringed in the chair on the other side of the room, holding the bible up before his face as though to hide behind it.

Avery stuck the tip of his pinky finger in his ear to try and clear out the instant tinnitus. "Guess nothin's changed then," he replied.

Morty stared at him, glanced at Rollie—who was shaking his head to get the echo out—then cleared his throat. "Really, she's a right trollop."

"Sounds like my mother," Avery replied. "She still a dope fiend, too?"

Morty hesitated for just a moment, then got that wicked grin on his face again. "Why don't you ask her yourself?"

Then his face shifted; the features seemed to soften, the two-day-old stubble receded, and, surprisingly, his skin darkened—not enough to pass as a black woman, but close enough so that Avery could actually see some similarity to his dead mother. It was when the eyes changed color which convinced him that, once again, he was in the presence of that damnable woman.

"Avery," said the voice that came out of Morty's mouth—and Avery would be damned if it didn't sound exactly like her.

"Pearl," he answered after a moment.

"You stupid sonuvaBITCH!" she screamed, fury contorting the features of Morty's face. There was hatred there—the same hatred he had seen in her face every time she had struck him or one of his siblings. Oh, the torment she had put them through, resenting them all for the same vile offense: being born. She had made their lives miserable by inflicting her misery onto them. From the daily berating's to the times when she was drunk enough to still connect when she swung at them. Pearl White had once had the meanest right hook in all of St. Petersburg, Florida, and she regularly enjoyed demonstrating the effects of her powerful punch on her children. That typically occurred around nine-thirty at night; anytime after that, and they could count on her missing. There had been many a night the children of the White household had shaken in fear, waiting for that particular time to arrive.

They would then watch the minutes tick by, each one an eternity, until enough time had passed that the fear would loosen its grasp on them for the breathing to become easier, and for the sweat to cease leaking from them like tears.

And now here she was, berating Avery again, and after he had put her in the ground nearly thirty years ago. That despicable, wretched woman, back to try and instill that same fear in him.

"You a waste of air, you numb little FUCK!"

How that voice used to haunt his dreams. That cadence, that same delivery she used whether she was sober or drunk. Always screaming the last word of her sentence, even if it wasn't an insult.

"Fetch me another goddamn BEER!" she would command.

"I told you mother fucka's to get you little asses to BED!"

"Who pissed on the damn seat of the TOILET?!"

All the same. Filled with anger and rage and hatred at the living results of her not being able to keep her legs together. Of the five children, only two shared the same father—and that was the twins, Maggie and Meg. And hadn't they gotten it worst of all? In one summer, Maggie had wound up with a broken arm, and Meg a broken jaw—on separate occasions, and months apart. Not that the law had time to spend on little beaten black children back in the 1920s; better to leave them at home, and let the law of averages sort them out. The cops had been no help to Avery and his siblings then, just as they were no help to his brethren nowadays. It was the 1980's, over sixty damn years later, and the only thing that had changed, so far as Avery could tell, was that they were allowed to vote, and could sit in the same dining room at restaurants. That was his experience, at least; although his sons and grandchildren had good jobs, had gone to college or were currently enrolled, Avery's personal experience had taught him too many lessons he never wanted his kin to have to learn.

"Are you listening to me, you SHIT?!" his mother screamed at him.

Only Avery wasn't a child any longer, was he? He was a man grown—more than that, he was a man *lived*, a man that had survived a war in Europe and worked hard to provide for a family that he loved, and buried one of his children after the Vietnam War, and walked his daughter down the aisle and helped to deliver his first grandbaby. He had lived and loved and made love and survived the goddamn Civil Rights Movement and even marched right alongside Andrew Young.

Morty glared at him with his mother's hateful eyes, lips peeled back in that hateful sneer of hers. "I shoulda smothered you in yo crib—"

"Bitch, PLEASE!" Avery yelled, and the Morty-mom flinched back. "You think I ain't heard all that before? Damn, woman, put the other guy back on! Least he wasn't a dried-up old whore with a soul full o' gunk and a heart full o' nasty, smelly-ass socks!"

She stared back at him, and then those female features began to slowly slip away. The darkness faded from Morty's face, the stubble poked back through, and his eyes went from hazel back to a deep blue.

Avery felt Rollie touch his shoulder, and he glanced at his friend to reassure him that he was okay, he was fine, he wouldn't be up late that night worried about his mother bursting into his room and trying to beat the everloving shit outta him.

But Rollie had other concerns on his mind. "Did you just quote the Grinch song?"

Avery shook off his hand and leveled a finger at Morty. "That the best you got, mother fucker? You need a minute?"

The possessed man stared at him, his mouth slightly open. "Uh...um, you're a dirty negro and he's a closeted fag?"

Both men took a step forward, but Avery was quicker to respond. "That's just plain offensive, asshole!" he said, pointing a finger accusingly at Morty.

The Morty-demon grinned in response. "Hit a nerve, did I?"

Avery was about to go on a tirade, but Rollie interrupted. "Actually, that was a pretty good one. Quick, too. That might be where your problem is: your delivery. You should have led with the derogatory names. I mean, no, I don't want to be called a 'fag', and I'm pretty sure that the word 'negro' is a bit outdated." He leaned forward, placing his hand to the side of his mouth as though to hide the next words from his best friend. "And I definitely would not go with that other 'n-word', because that's just tasteless, man.

"And you sound like you're from England—they're a lot more refined over there."

Morty looked at him doubtfully. "You'd be surprised actually. There is an awful lot of bigotry there, too."

"Were you ever one of them?" Rollie asked.

Morty shook his head vehemently. "For goodness sake no! I mean, sometimes I practice saying words like that, but it never sounds right when it comes out of me mouth."

"Well," Rollie replied, "therein lies your problem. You can't say those words convincingly enough. I'd go with something else next time. Also, you're trying to insult a bunch of old guys."

"Yeah," Avery said, stepping forward. "We've heard just about everything. Ain't nothin' you got what's gonna rile us up enough to hurt our friend Morty. But I gotta ask: how come you pick on the black guy first? That is pretty racist, man."

Morty sighed. "Because I've got nothing on him besides the gay thing," he said, nodding towards Rollie.

His friend shrugged his shoulders. "I was an only child in a strict Catholic household. My bad."

There came a light rapping on the door, and Ms. Marrow stuck her head in the room. "Everything okay in here, boys? Sounded like things were getting a bit heated."

"How's Miggs doing?" Avery asked her.

Ms. Marrow smirked. "Drooling on the couch."

Avery shook his head, and then Rollie both looked back at the Morty-demon. "Well, son?" Avery asked. "What are we doin' here? You ready to take a fuckin' hike?"

The possessed man sighed dejectedly. "I mean, I suppose so? It's all sort of pointless now, ennit?" He looked like he was about to cry, and Rollie had to fight the urge to comfort the poor man-demon.

Then Morty looked up at them sheepishly, a glimmer of hope in his eyes. "Unless you guys know of someone else I could possess?" Speaking the idea out loud seemed to reinvigorate him, and color returned to his pale face. "Seriously, mates, do a bloke a solid, yeah? I can't go back to Hell a failure and whatnot. Bloody Dukes o' Hell'll be up me arse if I don't strike a good bit o' fear in someone. Please?"

The two men glanced at each other, then shook their heads. Neither one was ready to commit themselves to that course of action—Avery because he was certain that choice would have him spending eternity having to listen to Pearl's irritating voice, and Rollie because the man did not have a spiteful bone in his body.

Paulo, on the other hand, had no reservations. If it would speed up the process and he could get back to his soaps, he had just the person. "Yeah, ya know, I'm thinkin' I got just the person," he said.

* * *

Once the ex-priest and the demon had ironed out the details—name, location, etc.—the demon had then advised him which page of the bible to read from.

No sooner had Paulo spoken the words than the demon said, "Right, yeah, that hurts, cheerio!" Then Morty had collapsed back on the bed, trembled violently a few times, and then was still, excepting for the rapid rise and fall of his chest as he sucked in lungfuls of air like a man saved from drowning.

Then he had looked at them each in turn and asked for them to explain just why the fuck he was tied up to his bed.

The following morning saw the trio at the Shady Palms Recreational Center, staring up at fat, yoga pants wearing asses. Avery was on all fours, pretending to try and get into some sort of pose. Morty, on the other hand, was holding Downward Dog longer than either man had thought possible.

"You sure you aren't possessed anymore?" Rollie asked him distrustfully.

Morty smiled and shook his head. "Nah. Just feel pretty damn limber today. Might hafta go give Ms. Marrow a call later," he said, and winked at Avery.

He snorted in return. "That woman would break you in half," he retorted.

"So where did the demon go?" Rollie asked, clearly not interested in the direction the conversation had taken. "Anyone we know?"

"No idea," Avery said. "All Paulo would say was that nobody was gonna fuck with Erica Kane anymore."

Morty looked over at him. "Who the hell is

Erica Kane?"

"Fuck if I know," Avery replied. "Anyway, we gonna keep doing this yoga shit? Because if that woman smiles when she says 'lotus' again, I'm callin' the Catholics in this time."

Rollie glanced up at the yoga instructor and studied her. Anna was in her late thirty's, had her hair pulled back in a severe ponytail, and was thick in the thighs and breasts. She was wearing a bright pink leotard with white leggings—she looked too damn shiny, and the visage made his eyes hurt.

"You think she's possessed, too?" he asked.

"She ain't possessed," Morty said, still holding that damn dog position that Avery hated so much. "And I'd know."

Just then, the instructor clapped her hands to get everyone's attention and smiled that thousand-watt smile of hers. "I'm excited to announce a new program tomorrow, ladies and gentlemen! Be sure to do your stretches before you get here!"

One of the older women near the front—Agnes, Avery thought her name was, although it could have been Ethel or Ruth, for all he cared—waved her arm excitedly, like a kid in a classroom that had to go to the bathroom before they pissed themselves.

"What is it?" she asked.

"It's called 'Sweatin' to the OLDIES'!" Anna the yoga instructor yelled.

The three men looked at each other, and

Avery gave a solemn nod.

"Better call Paulo," he said.

EPILOGUE

Captain's Log, stardate whogivesafuck.

I tied up the fucking traitorous bastard robot to a chair in the rec room. Well, it's more like I chained him there. And covered his eyes with duct tape because I got tired of the friggin' beady things staring at me anytime I walked in there.

And okay, yeah, I covered his entire head with the rest of the tape only after I found the screws that were holding it onto his frigging neck and took the fugging thing off.

And I mighta used it as a basketball a couple of times...look, the robot's head was shit as a soccer ball, and I was using the tape to help cushion it so I didn't break my fucking foot on the gorram thing. Sucked as a basketball too, though—didn't bounce worth shit. It might still be stuck in the hoop.

I stashed poor Johannsen in cold storage with the thing that was still sucking on his head so you science geeks at The Company can get a good look at it. I put 'em in the corner, beneath the vegetables. You know—the one area I won't be gettin' food from.

Already sent the message to his family, Gods rest his creepy little soul. He was a good First Mate, but damn if he didn't spend all his free time with porn on his dreamphones. Man has—er, had—quite the collection.

I got the other squid in my bunk. Turns out, the two that got in the cargo bay were much smaller versions of the big one that ate the five kegs. Not four kegs, like those traitorous bastards entered into the previous log—it was five. 'Cause they were planning on drinking one. Not me, though, I don't drink. That much.

So you guys get two specimens—the one that is part of the Johannsen-cicle, and the one I currently have in a container in my quarters. It's still alive, mostly due to the sacrifices I have made to keep it that way. Which means I should get to name it.

So the one I got in my locker—I mean to say, THE CONTAINER—well, that one doesn't have its teeth yet, so...I kinda had to improvise. If you guys need tips on how to feed it...tell you what, in case it kills me on the trip back, I'll just tell you. Hold the fucker with two hands when you feed it. That's all I'm saying...

Okay, look, I know it's gonna come up, so let me just clear a few things up. First of all, I figured out how to feed it ACCIDENTALLY. The thing had me cornered in the cargo bay, I tried jumping over it, I tripped, it jumped up and latched onto my pants...

Fuck it. Just...when you're feeding it, remember to use two hands, 'kay. Little fucker can get a bit... enthusiastic. If you hadn't made me get rid of my space hooker, I wouldn't be in this friggin' dilemma anyways.

And we're naming these fuckers 'space cookie monsters'.

Captain out, bitches.

ACKNOWLEDGMENTS

Behind every author, good or bad, there is that which helps make an environment comfortable enough to work in. Some need a dark room, complete quiet, or movies playing in the background. For me, its music. So the playlist for these stories included but is not limited to Lana Del Rey (of course), Peter Gabriel, The Fratellis, Chuck Berry, Aloe Blacc, and Eminem.

Several of the stories included here were written within the few months following my move to Maine. After not having written much fiction for the previous twenty-odd years, the change in locale proved to open a wellspring of sorts. Of course, I cannot testify to the quality of the work I produced, but I've tinkered with them for a few years, and they are as good as they're going to get--at least, for stories having been written by me...

Thank you to the entirety of the LeCrone and Bradford household, who gave me room to write for those first four months. Thanks to Kealeigh for her patience, Sophie for her shine, Christian and Marissa for their inspiration, and to Toby for proofing some of these and letting me know when I was using way too many parentheses. (it wasn't THAT many)(see what I did there?..) Also, a special thank you to Hobbes the cat for his particular indifference and excessive suaveness.

Thanks to James Austin, my Evil Editor at Tacitus Publishing for believing in some of these stories enough to include them in his previous anthologies. And for giving me a place to spout my weekly rants and reviews for a decade. And for letting me know when I was using too many commas, which was probably excessive at times (author's choice, I say), but never so much that the sentence went on, for like, an entire freaking page, if, you know, you know what I mean. (although I never used any commas within the parentheses, except for now)

Finally, thank you to my parents, and not just for doing ye olde slap and tickle and bringing me into the world in the first place. I inherited my mother's sense of humor (thank God) and my father's attention to detail—which could also explain why it takes me a long time to tell a joke, but dammit, I DON'T MISS ANY DETAIL IN THAT DAMN JOKE.

If you are still reading this, and if you enjoyed it, please leave a review on Amazon! We indie authors don't get a lot of press, and in this age of digital judgment, reviews are everything. And thank you for buying this book, for reading it, and for allowing me to entertain you, even if you were on the toilet while you were doing so. Nothing says quality time like a good movement, man.

For updates, general insanity, info on other books, and the occasional selfie, visit me here:

https://facebook.com/tskummelman/

I'm also on Twitter and Instagram:

twitter.com/tskummelman

instagram.com/tskummelman/

You can find my old film and TV reviews, plus assorted awesomeness, here:

facebook.com/TacitusPublishing/

I was going to get on Snapchat and that one where you swipe left or right depending on how desperate you think the other person is, but my daughter threatened to disown me, so, yeah...no swipeys.

ABOUT THE AUTHOR

T S Kummelman

lives in Maine and has two day jobs, but still finds time to write as he has no life and lives by himself. He is a movie buff, has a particular set of skills which would not aid him in any imaginable situation, is a part-time lunatic, and a full-time geek. Which could all explain why he hasn't had a proper date in decades...

www.ingramcontent.com/pod-product-compliance
Lightning Source LLC
LaVergne TN
LVHW091257150826
845673LV00006B/1455